Harper's Mother

Wendy Simons

HARPER'S MOTHER

Prentice-Hall, Inc.
Englewood Cliffs, New Jersey

Prentice-Hall International, Inc., London
Prentice-Hall of Australia, Pty. Ltd., North Sydney
Prentice-Hall of Canada, Ltd., Toronto
Prentice-Hall of India Private Ltd., New Delhi
Prentice-Hall of Japan, Inc., Tokyo
Prentice-Hall of Southeast Asia Pte. Ltd., Singapore
Whitehall Books Limited, Wellington, New Zealand
10 9 8 7 6 5 4 3 2 1

Library of Congress Cataloging in Publication Data
Simons, Wendy. Harper's mother.

Summary: Once again, Harper and her mother
leave the man with whom they've been living and
look for a new situation.
[1. Mothers and daughters—Fiction.
2. Single-parent family—Fiction]   I. Title.
PZ7.S605797Har 1980 [Fic] 80-17308
ISBN 0-13-383984-2

Editor's note: *The story takes place in New Zealand, which is in the Southern Hemisphere where the seasons are the reverse of those in the Northern Hemisphere. Some of the names of cities and towns mentioned in* Harper's Mother *can be traced back to the Maori, the original Polynesian settlers.*

Harper's Mother

· 1 ·

Seagulls screech, scraps of white linen soaring in the sky. Spray leaps up and engulfs us. We duck, mother and I. She shields me with the corner of her plastic raincoat but it does little good. I'm drenched. Salt water. Pickled. Corned beef smells with lots of cloves and whole onions. Carrots cooked in the brine. Cosy it was once with the coal range glowing and the house hermetically sealed against night ghosts. Perhaps it will be like that again one day when we settle somewhere.

I say, "I like corned beef. 'Specially in sandwiches."

"Do you?" she says. "Perhaps for your school lunch. . . ."

She doesn't bother to finish.

The sky is pinched gray in the fading light. Clouds romp puppy fashion. Another wave. Duck. In my hair this time and running down my face. I lick the salt water, curling my tongue upward toward my nose. I pretend it's snot like the little kids at school. I've seen them do it. With the real thing. The wind's cold. It cuts right through my plastic raincoat which is too small for me now. The sleeves don't reach to my wrists and my skirt hangs down below it. I can't do it up. The button holes are ripped and the buttons slide undone all the time. The wind makes my skin shiver. Little ripples run up and down me. My dress is wet and clingy.

"When will the bus come?" I say.

"Soon."

"Where're we going?"

1

"To town."

"Will we be coming back?"

"Here. Have another chip."

She holds it out between thumb and index finger. Cold it is, and greasy. The salt has melted into the fat. It weeps tears like my hair and the dribble down the back of my neck. I shake my head at her. It looks unappetizing and I don't want to eat it. She shrugs and throws it onto the footpath.

The seagulls swirl around, land, thrust out their necks and squawk. One, the aggressive one, darts at the others. Ugly cries of protest but they move away, sideways, crablike. The aggressive one picks up the chip and swallows it whole, its head down and forward, neck muscles struggling to cope with the sodden mess. I think it will choke.

It's supposed to be summer but the pohutukawa trees look gnarled and angry this evening. Their dark heads toss splatters of purple-red blood.

I wonder why we have to sit here at this bus stop instead of going to the one further down the road where there's a shelter, but I don't ask. She's in no mood for conversation. She's in her silent mood, thinking over the afternoon's peculiar circumstances which landed us here.

Thorn shouldn't have done it and then we wouldn't be sitting here with nowhere to go. It would be dinner time now. Stew with lots of vegetables and mashed potatoes to mop up the gravy. The television would be on so that we wouldn't have to make conversation about things we didn't want to say. If she hadn't caught us, I wouldn't have told but I hate him for it. Never liked him. The way he hung around outside the bathroom door trying to peek in at me. The way he looked with his empty eyes across the table, following my fork to my mouth, watching me chewing and how I licked the gravy from my chin, smiling pathetic smiles.

2

She noticed, too. Leering, she called it.

"Stop leering, Thorn," she'd say.

He'd look down then, chastised.

I asked him once who my real father was.

Grinned his lecherous grin, he did.

"Search me," he said, clutching the front of his trousers.

The plastic raincoat crackles as she lifts it over me. We bow our heads as though out of respect for something more powerful than we are. There's a clatter of small stone noises as the spray hits the coat and trickles downwards. I can see the silver threads of water descending on the outside of it if I stretch my eyes up high in their sockets. There's a brief cosiness, being close to my mother with little rivers snaking around us. Like being in a plastic cocoon. Then she straightens up and removes her arm from my touch.

"We must've just missed one," she says.

It was the way Thorn kissed me goodnight. Full on the lips and wet. I tried to avoid it.

"Going to bed now," I'd call from the lounge doorway.

My mother would look up briefly and say, "Goodnight, dear."

Thorn would leap up several quick strides toward me.

"How about a goodnight kiss for poor Uncle Thorn?" he'd say.

I'd offer a cheek. I'd been taught to be polite and he was supposed to be my uncle. When I was younger he used to cuddle and tickle me. Playfully, I thought. But not any more. He'd grip my head, hands closed over my ears, and jerk it around to face him. Close we were. Eyeballs almost touching. His hands strong as he ignored my resistance. Soundless his kisses, soft and sloppy. Sometimes a slap on the tail as I retreated.

I wonder what he's doing. Hope he's lonely. But he won't be yet. We've only been gone about an hour. In a day or two when he realizes we won't be going back. Then, I'm not sure . . .

"Are we going back?"

"Where?"

"Home. Uncle Thorn's place?"

"No. And he's not your uncle."

I know that already. Am relieved at being released from the burden of calling him uncle when I loathe him so much.

The traffic starts to flow. Car after car, lumbering trucks, and a bus like a moving home, curtains drawn back to show whoever wants to look—people suspended from the ceiling, rocking gently like the sausages at the delicatessen. Faces molded out of pale clay are pressed against the glass.

It's going the wrong way for us.

"Not long now," she says.

We left in a bit of a rush, and I've forgotten my toothbrush. It's on the shelf in the bathroom, sitting alongside his shaving gear. Forgotten my green cardigan, too, my only good one. Hope I can get them back. Things are crammed into my suitcase, screwed up, careless.

Did she bring the iron? We'll need it when we get to wherever we're going. I don't ask.

"We're leaving," she said. "Pack your things and hurry."

"When? Now?"

But she didn't answer. She was too busy swirling things up in her arms as she passed from one room to another. He followed but she said nothing directly to him. She was muttering. Angry.

"I've had enough. Don't think I haven't been watching you, you dirty brute. Don't think I haven't seen you ogling and leering at my daughter."

4

Suitcases tumbled from high cupboards. Possessions swept up and thrown in, pressed down, lids forced closed, and all the time he watched, leaning in doorways.

"Get out of the way," she'd said several times, elbowing past him and he'd stepped aside.

I was trembling as I snatched at useless things and stuffed them into my suitcase. Couldn't think what to take, what things I'd need most, as I had no idea where we were going, and all the time I could hear the shuffle of Thorn's slippers trailing her up and down the hall. A cripple, he seemed, whose crutch was about to be wrenched away from him. He was mute with astonishment and fear. And I felt fear in case he should come into my bedroom. It was reassuring to hear, in contrast, my mother's heels ringing out sharply the disgust and determination she felt as she strode around on the bare wooden floors.

No carpet in that house. It had just the bare essentials and, like a church hall, it was all wood panelling and high ceilings. Dim, too, inside, because of the bushes growing close to the windows, scratching on the glass when the wind blew, making creepy noises late at night when the lights were out and the house quiet—creaking iron on the roof and sudden cracks of timber like old bones grinding in their sockets. Bumpy it was outside, mostly dandelions and paspalm grass, with a hydrangea hedge separating the house from the vegetable garden.

Thorn came toward me behind the hydrangea hedge. He must have been watching to see me go around there.

"Look," he said, voice full of surprise, his trousers undone, his cock showing.

Close to me. Breathing heavily.

"Touch it," he said. "Like this."

Face flushed.

"Rub it," he said.

I didn't want to. It disgusted me. He repelled me with

5

perspiration sitting on his forehead and hot patches on his cheeks. His eyes were half-pleading, half-threatening me. No escape for me. I was cornered.

"Get out. Get away or I'll scream."

He laughed then.

"No you won't," he said gripping my arm, his fingers pressing into the bone. "Do as I say or I'll tell your mother about the cigarettes."

Frightened I was then. My fingers reached toward his open fly but I couldn't touch him.

"At last!" says my mother. "Take your suitcase and that box."

It comes lumbering toward us, headlights poised higher than the cars in the navy-blue evening. There's a sudden weight on my arms as I struggle across with the box and my suitcase. I heave them into the luggage compartment at the side and climb onto the bus where I stand foolishly dripping puddles at the entrance, suddenly shy as the glow of lights hits me. Eyes pierce my wet raincoat, my dress and my skin.

"Where to?" says the driver.

"City," says my mother.

Her elbow digs me and I'm propelled down the aisle. The bus starts up before we're seated and I fall. The seat is still warm from the person sitting here before me.

We move gently and the city cruises by. There are houses etched onto the backdrop sky with shiny boxes for eyes. The cranes on the waterfront remind me of birds described in science fiction books. There's something futuristic about the strength of all those weird shapes on the wharves. But we're secure in our moving rocket, lulled by the motion, snug within our own thoughts.

They were Thorn's cigarettes. We took them down to the embankment near the railway lines. Katie, Jennifer and I. We sat furtively behind a broom bush and fumbled with matches, white sticks protruding from between our lips. We probably looked ridiculous, but we felt grown-up except for the grains of fear huddled in our stomachs.

"What if someone catches us?"

"My father'd kill me."

I got the cigarette to light first. Didn't choke on the first puff or the second. Our fantasy worlds lifted us into a new adult one and it was fun. We did it as often as I could steal the cigarettes. It was our secret, something to counteract the secrets that the grown-up world held against us.

Thorn didn't seem to miss his cigarettes but he wasn't as casual about them as I thought. He must have been saving the knowledge up to use against me. He would've made a fuss, too, if he'd told my mother and she'd have been furious. Punishment then. Tingling bottom at the thought.

There were the expedients, the ear-twistings and legslappings which were painful enough but not as bad as the premeditated punishments. They were the ones I hated most. Like when I went through a cheeky stage and was always being shoved onto the veranda when it was dark. There were long cobwebs and fat black spiders and my thoughts were of rats gnawing at my stomach. Or there was the stage I went through when I had sloppy table manners and had to eat my food off newspaper under the table with the smell of hot feet to accompany it.

Harsh my mother is in some ways.

The worst time was when I said *bloody*. She was in one of her pure speech phases. She took the word up to teach me a lesson.

"Come and help with the bloody dishes," she'd say. "When you've finished you'd better do your bloody homework but before you do either of those things would you please put the bloody milk bottles out. We don't want to miss the bloody milkman."

It went on for a whole week and it was awful. Every time she

7

said it, the word would roll around in my head, thumping the inside of my skull.

There was always some hint of antagonism between Thorn and my mother. A niggle. Implied hostility. Suspicion rested at the backs of their eyes and when they looked at each other or touched, there was no spontaneity. Their actions were forced as though they were trying to convince themselves and each other that they belonged together.

She was different when we lived with Uncle Paul. She was rowdy then, impulsive and uninhibited, quick to anger and quick to laugh. With Thorn she was quieter, going through the motions of caring but always seeming to retain some private resource—in case of disaster. And Thorn, aware of her reserve, was reliant on her, doggedly devoted.

At the beginning, it had been tolerable, living with Thorn. It was about two years ago when we moved into his house. All summer, every weekend, we went somewhere. A different place each time. We would pore over district maps every Friday night, arguing, planning the weekend campaign. Off to the dairy, running furiously with the large shopping basket banging against my legs, anxious to get there before closing time. Bread for sandwiches, bags of tomatoes, thick blocks of cheese, oranges or peaches or plums. Loud-voiced, I'd tell the shopkeeper and any customers who happened to be there why I was shopping so late:

"We're going to the beach tomorrow. Spratt's Bay. On the bus." or "It's Cherry Island where we're going this weekend. On the eight-fifteen ferry. We'll have to wake up early."

Sunburned days they were. Me, red, flecks of skin peeling off my nose and shoulders, in and out of the sea, straddled in the hot sand. My mother, sunglassed and magazined, spread the scent of her suntan lotion across the beach. Thorn, trouser legs

8

rolled to the knees, shirt sleeves up, would sit in the shade for fear of burning. Pale skinned, conspicuously white, he appeared an alien in our sundrenched world.

Then there were the walks in the evening to catch the bus, me in between them, one hand in each of theirs. More food, with the kitchen door open and the cicadas purring their ceaseless ululations. The birds would be making their goodnight overtures. The sun would be pale and weary. Sleep for me, deep, long and soothing.

We always ate boiled eggs for breakfast on Sunday mornings, me sitting between them tapping at the rounded head. I felt mischievous, wanting to continue my tapping in rhythmical movement over to Thorn's head. He was bald, smooth like the thick end of the egg. I wondered whether his bald patch would shatter, too, if I tapped it with the base of my spoon. Silent laughter inside me at the thought.

Winters always seem to be wet. We were confined in Thorn's house, physically close, with the rain and sludge making prisoners of us. The long dreariness of weekends was punctuated by my mother's sharp comments, her reluctant meals, her irritation at Thorn's presence.

It was then that he became aware of me in a different way, watching me silently over the newspaper and appearing outside my bedroom door. Sometimes I'd creep to the door and, flinging it open, would catch him there. Startled, he'd grin foolishly and scuttle away like some skinny-legged spider.

Me? Bored. There were things to do, jobs for my mother, for example, but nothing that interested me. I'd wander from room to room, window gazing at the desolate garden, daydreaming.

I knew she was beginning to get tired of Thorn. I could see the resistance in her shoulders, the shudders when he went too close to her. Her voice was clipped when she spoke to him and she bossed him.

"Don't do that Thorn," she'd snap.

"For goodness sake, Thorn," and her eyes would rise heavenward in exasperation.

She treated him like a child. Sometimes it seemed that she considered him younger than me. Her eyes were watchful, too. Alert to his growing obsession with me, knowing that he was hanging around the bathroom door, bounding in to catch me naked or half-dressed, conscious of his crude jokes about my underwear and the wet goodnight kisses. Waiting to pounce, she was, still as a cat. I know the pattern. She'll tolerate so much, my mother, and then she's had enough. There's no compromise, no remission or forgiveness then.

"We're leaving," she'd say and suitcases would materialize, lids open, belongings would be crammed in, and off we'd go, laden like pit ponies in search of another home.

The bus turns sharply into the narrow alley leading to the terminal. We roll drunkenly, my mother crushing me against the window. People awaken and move reluctantly down the aisle toward the door.

"Not far now," my mother says.

"Where're we going?"

"You'll see. To a boarding house."

It's raining. Angry summer rain pelts down on us. No protection from her raincoat this time. We're too intent on arriving at the boarding house, arms stretched to the ground, groaning under the weight of our luggage. Breath short. Pain under my ribs and in my throat. My eyes sting. I feel like grizzling as tired babies grizzle.

"Why did we have to leave tonight? I'm soaked and my arms hurt?" I say.

We've stopped for shelter under the veranda of a shop. It has saddles in the window, heavy hunks of arched leather and spurs that glisten softly under the glow of the window lighting. It reminds me of "The Virginian," the program I hate to miss.

"You know perfectly well," she snaps.

She's tired, too. Perhaps wearied by our incessant shifting around like modern day gypsies.

"God this weather's terrible," she says.

Strange shapes glide past us. Phantom people they are, with collars high and heads pulled into their shoulders. Some show no interest in us, as though we aren't here, but others peer at us, partially curious, partially threatening. A drunk man lurches toward us, weaving from one side of the sidewalk to the other. He's muttering, caught in the web of his private, befuddled thoughts.

"Come on," says my mother.

We gather our luggage, she pushing me protectively to the inside, shop edge of the footpath.

I try to count the number of times we've shifted but I'm so weary I keep losing count. I miss some out and when I go back to gather them up, become muddled. I'm hungry. Didn't eat the fish and chips earlier because my stomach was churning from the sudden outlandish events that precipitated our flight.

We drag on up the street, cold, absorbing the loneliness of the deserted city center.

"This'll do," says my mother, veering left suddenly.

There's a neon sign which blinks *Keyes' Private Hotel* at us. Below it a board bangs against a post. It says that there are vacancies. We climb the steps and enter a dim hall, one naked bulb casting opaque light in a honey-colored circle. It reminds me of the hall at Thorn's place, high-ceilinged and empty. There's a cubby hole at one side and a stairway at the rear. A wooden arm juts out at us. *Office* it says. The door on the right is closed but black lettering tells us it's the dining room.

I stand, miserable, isolated in my pool of rain water. The

woman inside the cubby hole looks up. She has a thick black moustache. Her upper arms wobble but she smiles, and it's like a glimpse of the sun after a week of rain.

My mother signs a book and the proprietress takes a key from a pigeon hole.

"Leave that to me, sweetheart," she says and, moving with extraordinary agility for such a large woman, she comes into the hall and takes one of my suitcases.

We struggle up the stairs, her continuous chatter falling about me like pebbles.

"We're here now," my mother whispers encouragingly behind me.

My legs ache. I feel like a machine, working mechanically under the control of someone else, moving, not because of my own free will, but because of some motivating force remote from me but in command of my reflexes. Tears well in my eyes. My legs and arms and shoulders will break, I think.

"Here we are," says the woman fiddling with a key in the lock. "It's a small room but comfortable."

She flings the door open and, in a sudden burst of energy, fluffs around patting the beds, straightening the bath towels, reassuring us of the comforts contained within her establishment.

"The bathroom's down the end of the hall," she says. "Ladies on the right. But you have your own handbasin and there's plenty of hot water. Breakfast's between seven and eight. No room service, I'm afraid. We're only a small establishment. Permanents mainly."

There's a pause. She's waiting for someone to take the cue, to make the appropriate noises. Then she realizes how tired we are. She chucks me lightly under the chin.

"Straight into bed with you, sweetie," she says.

"It's very nice. Just what we want. Thank you," says my mother.

"Well, then, if there's nothing more I can do for you I'll say goodnight. You'll be comfortable I'm sure. It's a very quiet house," says the lady. Her hand rubs the door knob. "Sleep well," and she closes the door after her.

Exhaustion. Confusion. I stand weeping silently. My mother helps me undress.

"Come on, in you get," she says, holding back the bed-clothes.

The mattress is innersprung, the sheets crisp, clean laundered. I sink and the tension comes out in a long sigh. My mother's thumbs lightly press my eyelids. Her lips touch my forehead.

· 2 ·

"Hello."

"Hello, Harper. You're awake, dear?"

There she is, my mother, dressed and sitting astride the bed, one leg tucked under her body, the other stretched out. Her reading glasses hang on the end of her nose. She always wears them that way when she's feeling businesslike. The morning paper's open in front of her at the classified section.

Someone in the house is running a tap, and the pipes outside our window groan with the effort of transporting water.

"Those pipes make a heck of a noise," I say.

She laughs.

"Worse than Thorn's snoring."

Even though the curtains are drawn across, I can tell it's a fine day. The room's warm from the chinks of sunlight filtering through where the curtains hang short of the sill. It's a faded pink and beige room with the beds high off the floor and the wardrobe a neat fit at the bottom of my bed. The lightshade's subdued with dust.

I screw up my eyes and make faces out of the brown water stains that blotch the ceiling. There's a round jowly face of an old woman, the skinny profile of a man with a sharp hooked nose but with an eye missing, and a child with one large, one small ear. My eyes follow the beading between the wall and ceiling, slide down one of the faded stripes on the wallpaper and rest on my mother's downturned head. Her index finger is running down the columns of the newspaper, pausing every now and then. Large blue ballpoint crosses mark the margin.

"What're you doing?" I say.

She doesn't look up.

"Trying to find somewhere to live."

"Found anything?"

"One or two possibilities." She looks over at me. "Hungry?"

"Ravenous."

"Better get up then. No one's going to wait on you while you lounge there."

"No room service!" I say, mimicking the proprietress, and my mother laughs.

I make no move. There's security in the small room. A feeling of languidness, indifference to the world outside.

"It's seven thirty," says my mother looking at her watch. "Only half an hour before the dining room closes."

She's mellow this morning. Softer. The gravel's gone out of her voice and she smiles. It's a long time since I've seen her this way. She's always like it when we leave somewhere, as though an enormous weight has been lifted from her back and she can straighten up at last. Like it at the beginning, too, when we first go to live somewhere new. Then it creeps in, the irritation, the intolerance when I can't seem to do anything that pleases her. She always starts by finding fault with me, and then gradually her displeasure spreads to include the other person. 'We'll be leaving soon,' I think.

"Did you bring the iron?" I say.

"Heavens above," she says. "There's no time for ironing. Hurry up. I'm starving. I'll fade away if I don't eat soon."

My dress is crumpled, still damp and salty from the dousing it got last night. I shiver slightly as I pull it on. Lying flat on my

15

stomach, I reach under the bed for my sandals, then fling water over my face and comb my hair in a cursory fashion. Hunger makes me careless.

"Ready," I say.

At the bottom of the stairs we meet the proprietress.

"Good morning," she beams. "Hello, sweetheart. Did you have a good sleep?"

Her eyes rove over my body and some of the affability goes out of them as she takes in my grubby and crumpled dress. She withdraws slightly and I immediately feel that I'm not a suitable guest for her boarding house. I wish I'd put something else on. My mother slings an arm over my shoulder, a casual gesture but protective. She's noted the woman's disapproval, too.

"This way."

The woman has become abrupt. She indicates a table in the middle of the room. There's a man sitting there.

"We're setting up for lunch," she says. "Do you mind sharing?"

She gives us no choice.

The man we are to share with looks up briefly and says good morning. There's something odd in the look. I feel apprehension and draw my chair closer to my mother's. Then he looks at me full faced and smiles. I can feel the flush of embarrassment rising from my neck to smear my face red. He has an artificial eye. I look quickly around the room, wanting to be freed from the awful, compelling fascination of his lopsided gaze.

There's a woman sitting by the window, alone, the newspaper folded neatly atop a silver vase. I concentrate on her. She eats absentmindedly but fastidiously, little fingernails bright red, hooked away from her knife and fork. Her hair is tinted and crimped into neat curls, lacquered as though doused in clear varnish. She's the only other person in the dining room now, but obviously it hummed with hungry people before we arrived.

16

The tables are in various stages of being cleared and reset. Tablecloths devoid of cutlery display fragments of the morning's activities. They're stained—coffee drips, blobs of marmalade, egg yolks, crumpled napkins, toast crumbs. . . .

The proprietress thumps two plates down in front of us. They contain tinned apricots. Two halves and a slither for me, three halves for my mother.

"You don't get much," the man with the false eye chuckles, "but it's edible."

I don't look at him.

"We're far too hungry to complain," says my mother.

I drag my spoon carefully around the side of the dish, gathering the last drops of syrup. An arm reaches over my shoulder and whips the plate away. I just have time to drop the spoon into it before it disappears.

It's bacon and egg next, and chips. The bacon's brittle, the chips and egg lukewarm. They've been in a warming drawer for some time.

"You've got to be down early," says the man. "Everything's cooked at the same time here. Mrs. Keyes does the breakfasts on her own."

Again I avoid looking at him.

"Mrs. Keyes?" says my mother.

"The lady waiting on the tables. She's the owner."

"Oh," says my mother. "We'll remember to be down early tomorrow then. If we're still here."

She looks across and smiles at him. She's not embarrassed.

"Are we leaving today then?" I say.

"We'll see," she says.

There's toast, too, bendy and hard to cut. The coffee's in a silver jug, the milk already in it. It's hot.

I want to ask whether I'll be going to school but I don't like to in front of the man. He might think it an odd question. He folds

17

his napkin, pushes back his chair and says, "Excuse me. Perhaps I'll see you at lunch time." He smiles at us both and I feel the infuriating redness creeping over my face again.

When he's gone, I say, "Will I be going to school? I can easily catch a bus out."

"Don't be silly," says my mother. "It's too late. Anyway, it's not safe."

"Why? What do you mean it's not safe?"

"Oh nothing. Here, eat this last piece of toast."

I know what she means. She's afraid of Thorn. Afraid that he'll be watching for me on the way to school or on the way home, lurking somewhere, his eyes soft with the thought of impending pleasure but determination behind them, a hardness because of his desire. I know the look. Seen it many times.

"Won't there be trouble if I don't go?" I say.

"Just for a couple of days? You could be sick."

The proprietress comes to our table. She asks whether we enjoyed our breakfasts and whether she can get us anything more.

We both say, "Yes, thank you. No, thank you."

"Come on, dear," my mother says. "They want to clear the table."

She's gone out now, newspaper under her arm, handbag jammed with addresses from the *Home Help Wanted* column.

"You stay here," she said. "No use the two of us going and wasting money on bus fares. Do some school work in the lounge if you like and I'll bring you something nice back. Be good." She kissed me. "Won't be long."

She'd cleaned her shoes, heels neatly polished, moving like twins. Extra care she's taken over her hair and makeup. Looks quite nice when she spends time on herself.

18

I worry about not going to school. There was trouble over it once when we lived on the dairy farm out of Kerrisville. She was housekeeper to Uncle Paul, then. That was before we met Thorn. I was only seven.

Uncle Paul's house was big and rambling but warm. It smelt slightly of cows, dogs and gumboots. Of roast dinners, earth and bottled fruit. Of fresh milk, newly dug potatoes and wood fires. There were Jersey cows ceaselessly eating grass down on the river flat, their tails flashing at flies which landed on their flanks, wandered over them, bit into them. Hour after hour I watched them, dawdling among them, considering them my friends as they gazed at me with soft, slightly astonished eyes. Sometimes I would lie on my stomach in the grass near the river with Hank the dog, watching their udders swelling with the milk that later we'd siphon off into the big stainless steel vats ready for the milk tankers.

We were free, Hank and I. Me hanging upside down from the apple trees, body swaying, sloth-like. Hank, resigned to waiting, would lie flat, head on the ground, eyes half-closed but fixed on me to make sure I didn't escape.

They were haymaking days. Big machines eating up the land. scones and tea for the workers, flecks of hay in my hair and up my nose. Sneezes.

In the winter it was feeding out time. My mother drove the tractor while Uncle Paul and I balanced on the trailer, pushing off bales of hay. Cows trailed like ribbon behind us.

The winters were heavy with fog, breath huffing like steam out of a kettle. Damp ground everywhere with globules of mud sticking to our gumboots. The orchard was churned up, the vegetable garden, soft pats of mud, brown and viscous, lying on the back lawn, mysteriously getting into the house. Sharp words from my mother then. Uncle Paul and I careful with our gumboots, scraping the mucilaginous blobs off at the fence, wobbling on the edges of their soles to the back door where we'd pull them off. Rain, too, in winter, often and heavy. Sad everything looked. The trees, leafless, stood like the cows; bent backs to the downpours. The dogs, slinking into their kennels, would curl tight, shivering. But there were fires for us. The coal range burnt steadily, glowing orange warmth. The kitchen was heavy with the mixed smells of drying clothes on the rack, corned beef, onions, faint cow odors. . . .

Then one day the letter came from the Education Department. Why wasn't I at school, they wanted to know. None of their business I heard my mother say to Uncle Paul. They argued about it.

"She needs it," he said. "She's getting out of hand. It's about time someone knocked her into shape."

"Rubbish!" snapped my mother. "There's enough education here for any kid. And I don't need criticism from you. You've been picking on her lately."

"I have not," he said. "The government provides free education and every kid's got to go."

"You just want to get rid of her," said my mother.

"Don't accuse me of ulterior motives, and stop reading things into my conversations that aren't there," Uncle Paul said. "I didn't say anything of the sort and you know it."

"You implied it. And you'd better get this straight right now. Harper doesn't do anything unless I say so."

"You're being bloody pigheaded," he said. "There'll be trouble if she doesn't go."

"I know you. You want her out of the way, that's all." Her voice sounded vicious.

"Oh Christ!" he said, exasperated. "I didn't realize how bloody stupid you are."

"Don't you call me stupid!"

Angry she was then.

"You are stupid. I'm taking her in on Monday whether you like it or not."

"You'll do no such thing," said my mother and there was menace in her voice.

The halcyon days continued for me. Had my eighth birthday, but it went without celebration and I didn't go to school. Quiet they'd become, my mother and Uncle Paul, working side by side in the shed. They didn't yell at each other over the hum of the machine and the clatter of cows' feet on concrete. Their eyes didn't meet and they no longer smiled at each other. Tense, my mother, eyes narrowed, lips stretched into that familiar thin line, and she picked on me.

We had the radio on at meal times to fill the space of their silence. Uncle Paul began going out, leaving the two of us to rattle around in the emptiness of his house. Late at night I'd hear his car joggling up the driveway, the headlights painting brief yellow lines across the ceiling. Weekends, too, he left us at home. Once we used to go to town to the football game or to the pictures. It all stopped. Suddenly.

One day the Truant Officer came to the house. Why wasn't I at school, she wanted to know. Did my mother know that it was illegal to keep me away? There was talk of prosecutions, summonses, magistrates' courts, welfare officers. I would have to live with someone else who knew how to look after me properly, she said. Someone who knew to send me to school every day. My mother conceded defeat and I was registered at the local school.

Every day I caught the bus at the gate, my packet of sandwiches crammed in beside books and my new sandshoes for sports. I went willingly, convinced that the guilt I felt at causing the rift between them would vanish. I thought things would improve. But they didn't.

Early one morning, before it was properly light, Uncle Paul came home and they had a fight. I stood shivering in my bedroom, listening, rigid with surprise and fear. There was yelling and swearing. My mother cried. It was over, our living with Uncle Paul. I wept to be leaving Hank.

"Why do we have to leave?" I asked her.

"Mr. Travers is getting married," she said.

"But why do we have to go?"

She didn't answer.

He drove us to the railway station. They didn't speak. Before we boarded the train he offered her money. She took it.

"I'm sorry," he said.

He kissed me goodbye.

It's hot in the lobby. No one has bothered to open a window and I don't know whether I should. It isn't really a lobby as in the big hotels, it's a porch that has been glassed in. The furniture's cane with heavy rubber cushions. I like the pattern on the fabric. It's swirly, sea-green and white like rushing water. I'm the only one here. There's a blowfly buzzing against the window sill. Its body looks psychedelic in the sunlight and its noise is deafening, muffling out the city sounds. I open my school case but there's nothing much I want to do in it so I close it and pick up a magazine from a side table. The table top is glass, smudged with the minute lines of damp fingers. A woman comes in with a vacuum cleaner. Haven't seen her before. She's thin with white calves.

"Not at school today?" she says, smiling at me.

My heart flips. Perhaps she'll tell the Truant Officer.

"I'm not very well," I lie.

22

"Aren't you, dear?"

She pauses and scrutinizes my face.

"It's better to stay quiet then, isn't it?"

She plugs the vacuum cleaner into the wall.

"If I'm in the way I can go to our room," I say.

"You're not in the way," she says, beginning to dust with a soft yellow cloth.

The glass table top is hard to clean. As she rubs it, it squeaks.

"Silly these tables in a place like this," she says. "You're not here on your own, are you, love?"

"No," I say. "My mother's here, too. She's gone out."

"Are you on holiday?"

"No."

"Not on holiday. Well! You are a lucky girl."

She taps her chin, head cocked and waits for an explanation. I don't reply. The magazine has suddenly become a refuge from her prying.

"Where's your mother gone?" she says at last.

"I'm not sure."

"Is your father here, too?"

Patronizing now, speaking as though I'm mentally handicapped.

"No," I say.

Sympathy on her face. I can see that she thinks we've run away.

"Where's your dad? What'd he do?" Her voice is unable to disguise her enjoyment in sordid gossip.

I shrug. I can't think what to say.

"You mean he's de. . . ?"

"Oh no," I say. "I haven't got one. At least I . . . I don't know . . . who. . . ."

I stop, blushing with confusion. The woman is embarrassing me.

23

"Oh," she says, "I see."

Death has been flushed out of her mind.

"Never mind, love," she says.

Her hand plunges into her smock pocket and she produces a packet of Arrowmint chewing gum which she gives me.

Mrs. Keyes comes in. Her eyes look fierce.

"Mrs. Carter," she says, "haven't you finished in here yet? And fraternizing with the guests. This child is a guest, believe it or not."

Mrs. Carter doesn't turn on the vacuum cleaner. Instead she follows the proprietress out the door. I can see them talking through the glass panes. Several times they look my way. Serious, their conversation, and I know it's about me. *Poor child. Such a shame. Looks so neglected. It's a disgrace. These solo mothers. Cluck cluck . . . cluck cluck. . . .*

It doesn't bother me. I thumb through the magazine, chewing my gum.

· 3 ·

The morning seems long. The magazines are few, tattered and not very interesting. There's one on gardening, on how to prune roses for best results, the building of small ponds and how to lay out an asparagus bed. I'm not interested in reading them. The print's too small and the words too technical. I look at the pictures. In a woman's magazine I find diversion. At the back there's a section entitled *Life's Problems* where people write in about their sexual, marital and other worries. I read these letters avidly, biting my fingernails, no longer aware of the blowfly on the window sill or Mrs. Carter's steady movement over the carpet behind with the vacuum cleaner. Pretend she isn't there so we don't speak.

I read about the problems people have with body hair, about white discharges from the vagina, and the dangers of withdrawal. Don't know what that means. The last letter fascinates me:

"I know that my husband loves another man. He loves this man as deeply and emotionally as a woman can love a man. You will probably tell me that homosexuality is normal and natural. How can I accept this when I am trying to bring up a teenage family who now look at their father with suspicion as I did before I realized the truth? How can I explain to them that their father no longer loves me but is deeply involved with another man? Please help me to cope with the humiliation of seeing my

25

husband's affections poured onto his boyfriend and advise me how to protect my children from homosexuality."

So that's what it's called, this love between two men. I know about it because I once caught Eric kissing another man. My mother used to get angry. She didn't like Eric being homosexual.

After we left Uncle Paul, we went to live with Eric. My mother knew him from somewhere in her past. He was rich. We lived in a penthouse high above the city. The carpets were thick, the chairs as soft as new mown hay so that we sank a long way down into them. The bathroom was tiled and had large windows overlooking the city. I liked sitting in the bath, soap-covered, watching the beetle-like cars, their movements slowed by the distance between us.

When we first arrived there, in the evening, all disheveled and gritty from the train ride, Eric wasn't pleased to see us. He frowned when he opened the door and asked my mother abruptly what she wanted. For a moment, I thought he was going to pretend he didn't know her. My mother answered briefly that we wanted to stay awhile because we had nowhere to go. Eric said that it was impossible.

"You've a spare room," my mother said. "There's no one else here."

She'd checked on that before we arrived.

Cliff-like, her face. Solid and determined. But then, I don't imagine it was easy for her to walk off the street and to knock on someone's door to ask if we could live with them. It was probably the embarrassment that made her aggressive.

Eric said, flustered, butterfly hands, "But, Kitty, we made a bargain. . . ."

"I need help," said my resolute mother. "You owe me . . . us . . . something. A few days accommodation until I find a place. Surely that isn't too much to ask."

She was bullying him. He shuffled backwards under her glare but still hung onto the door. He could have, at any time, slammed it closed. She hadn't cowed him, but he was bending. Silence while they summed each other up.

Then, "All right. Come in," Eric said.

We went in. And stayed. For months.

After a while, when Eric got used to us being there and got to quite like me, he gave my mother money to buy me clothes. It was fun visiting the big department stores, feeling the silk of the fabrics, the coolness of real leather, rubbing my face into the fur which lined expensive coats, parading, ridiculous in front of full-length mirrors and splitting our sides with laughter. My mother had become posh, her head held higher than before when we lived on the farm. Her voice was full, too, vibrating with correct pronunciation.

Parcelled, we'd feel sudden pangs of hunger, so—coffee bars among the chic office girls and dallying shoppers. Cool, dark these places with rows and rows of scrumptious food. Eyes popping, mouth watering, I'd wander up and down shelves, pondering, finding choices difficult to make. Our plates would be laden—cakes, sandwiches, bulging tarts. Busily, we consumed our food. I grew plump in those days.

"Good heavens child!"

I jump. Sudden fright. Mrs. Carter is twisted around so that she can peer at the magazine.

"You shouldn't be reading that rubbish," she says.

I blush.

"I don't really understand it," I say.

I fling the magazine away as though it's a hot iron burning my fingers.

"Haven't you got something else to do?" she says.

"Oh, yes," I assure her. "Lots."

I open my school bag eagerly, indicating that I'm well occupied, suitably interested in the contents.

"That's better," she says smiling approval. "When will your mother be back?"

There's censure in her voice.

"Soon," I say. "You musn't worry about me. I'm quite happy."

"You're a good girl," she says.

I thumb lethargically through the English textbook. It's boring. Mrs. Carter gathers up the vacuum cleaner and leaves. I'm glad she's gone. The sun's soothing as it filters through the glass panes. Pulling my legs up under me on the couch, puff the cushions around my head and close my eyes. I feel drowsy.

Eric was tall. Thin. Soft his eyes and kind to me. My mother and I shared a bedroom, the smaller of the two. Eric's bedroom was pink, a vibrant sunset pink with roses on the walls and a silky bedspread, shot Thai silk, smooth as the river pools on the farm. It smelt of jasmine. I liked to watch him. His movements were so graceful and he talked with his hands. They waved through the air, moving rhythmically like a conductor's baton, nails perfectly manicured. I tried to emulate him, striding through the apartment, hips waggling, hands fluttering, head thrown back so that my neck was arched like the rippling muscles of a horse as I laughed deep liquid sounds. Practiced in front of the mirror when my mother was out, trying to reproduce his mannerisms exactly.

Affected, people called him, his head cast on one side. Gentle, though, with his beautiful things, handling them with care—the Lladro figurines, the Waterford crystal, the alabaster ashtrays, the carved ivory figures with faces crinkled like screwed-up paper—caressed them, spoke softly to them as though they were his children, moved gracefully among them, long delicate strides, lace and falling water and piano music. Beautiful he was and I hold him somewhere near my heart with the same care with which he handled his ornaments, because he was careful with people, too, caressing them with his voice, his touch, his concern, as though we were created out of finest porcelain.

His eyes were enormous, a strange pale green, reflecting the different moods of his exquisite belongings.

Like my eyes, I think.

Suddenly, urgently, I must check out my eyes. There's a small convex mirror on the wall above the glass-topped table. Standing on tiptoes, I peer into it. It does strange things to my face. My cheeks look blown out as though I have a mouth bulging with water. My forehead has receded a long way into the distance and my eyes are almost oblong in shape. Can't see my true reflection but the color's there, the strange green of Eric's eyes. But not quite. Mine have flecks of yellow; the speckled yellow of late autumn apples.

I feel deflated. I want Eric's eyes.

The glass doors swing open and the proprietress comes in. She hasn't changed since that morning. Her look is severe and her arms wobble. I cower a little. She doesn't approve of me. As she sweeps in she's accompanied by a rich smell of stewing meat, cabbage, detergent—a strong kitchen smell. She's surrounded by an aura of polish and unsettled dust.

"It's lunchtime," she says. "Are you meant to be eating here?"

I shrug, nod and then shake my head.

"What does that mean?" she says. "Is your mother back yet?"

"No," I say, "but she'll be back soon."

"You'd better come and have some lunch," she says.

I suspect her of thinking of our money.

29

"It's all right," I say. "Thank you. I'll have some lunch when my mother gets back."

"The dining room closes at one sharp," she says.

She looks at me thoughtfully. Her eyes travel over my skinny legs, my concave stomach. They rest on my face. Her scrutiny reminds me of the time I was weepy and had no energy. My mother took me to the doctor. He looked at me in the same way and prodded me with his lukewarm finger—the way I prod at earthworms. I squirm under Mrs. Keyes' gaze and she thaws a little.

"Come on with me," she says. She sighs and speaks more to herself than to me. "It's ridiculous to leave a child on her own all morning. Can't understand some parents."

I want to protest but she has turned as if retreating. She pauses at the swing doors.

"Come along. Hurry up, dear," she says. "I haven't got all day."

I'm reluctant but follow.·

"In you go," she says, pushing the dining room door open. "You know the place. Same as this morning."

She leaves me, and I realize that I must sit with the man with the artificial eye. I move unwillingly into the room. It is fuller than at breakfast time and, although I don't look, I'm sure people are watching me. It is embarrassing knowing that their forks are suspended halfway to their mouths, food cooling, eyes boring holes in me as I make my way to the center of the room. The feeling is the same as that awful time when I first went to school and was too scared to ask the teacher if I could go to the toilet. Eyes, hard as marbles, seemed to watch me as I piddled down my legs, feeling the warm liquid flowing and, seeing with horror, dark spots appearing on the wooden floor. There was no sound in the classroom until my humiliation became so acute that I burst into tears.

30

Now I want to hurry and sink into a chair, to go puff under the handkerchief of a magician and disappear. I feel angered that my mother has abandoned me at such a time, that she could subject me to this humiliation. Sliding into the chair, I don't look at the man but am aware that he rises slightly from his seat.

"Hello, young lady. By yourself?" he says.

His voice is pleasant. I answer but don't look at him.

Mrs. Carter comes to my side. She's in a white smock now, her face set into the long-chinned look of disapproval that she wore this morning when she was talking to Mrs. Keyes about me.

"Hello, love," she says. "Mother not back yet?"

She clucks her tongue. I feel her giving a knowing look over my head at the one-eyed man and hope she meets his glass eye.

"Soup, love?"

"Yes, please," I say.

I don't want soup but don't know whether there's anything else. It's thick and lukewarm. I drink it without looking up. Nervousness makes me spill some. It dribbles down my chin.

"And how have you spent the morning?" the man says. "Had a pleasant time?"

I must look up at him.

I do.

"Reading."

I duck.

"Reading, eh? What were you reading?"

"School books," I say, head in plate.

There's curry next, dark brown, rich smelling, sitting on a bed of rice.

"I've been to the optometrist," he says. "I'm having a new eye made."

"That's nice," I say.

I'm trying to be polite—pleasantly interested—but it's dif-

31

ficult when I'm afraid of looking at the person speaking to me.

"Shall I tell you about it?" he says.

Doesn't he know how I feel?

"Oh no," I blurt. "Honestly. Things like that . . . like . . . your . . . well, you know. Those sorts of things don't worry me. I hardly notice them."

I'm furious that my face is hot, and, I imagine, red. The backs of my legs are wet against the chair. My hands are so slippery that I can hardly hold the knife and fork. I'm terrified that he's going to wiggle the painted orb out of his socket and offer it to me to touch.

"There's no need to feel embarrassed," he laughs. "It's been with me most of my life. I forget that some people are sensitive about it."

"Not me," I say, bravado, chin on chest. And to prove it, "How did it happen?"

"Are you sure you want to know?"

He's teasing me, but not unkindly so.

"I don't mind."

"I fell on a stick, when I was a youngster. That's all."

My stomach contracts at the awful thought. I can see him, stabbed through the eye like a fish on a spear. He goes on eating as though he's been telling me the latest weather forecast.

"Did it hurt?" I say, curiosity overcoming my revulsion.

"I suppose so. I can't really remember now."

He wipes his mouth on his napkin, leans back in his chair and looks at me.

"Did you know that the eye socket changes shape every so often?" he says. "Your eye coloring fades a bit, too, as you grow older. And you shrink. That's why I have to get a new eye."

"Have you ever had a different colored one?" I say looking at

32

his artificial eye which doesn't seem so frightening, so obscene, now.

"No," he says. "Always blue."

"It'd be fun to have a whole lot all different," I say. "You could wear a new one every day. You know, to match your shirts. That'd be neat."

He chuckles at me, genuinely amused.

"A blue one on Monday, green one Tuesday, pink on Wednesday, and white on Sunday, eh?"

We're friends. I tell him about my mother, about Eric, but not what I discovered in the magazine this morning. I talk of Thorn and giggle about the cigarettes, but don't tell him about what happened behind the hydrangea bushes. We talk about farming and Uncle Paul's place.

Comfortable I feel with him. Relaxed, because he doesn't 'tich-tich' at the number of places we've lived in. Nor does he poke to find out more about me. There doesn't seem to be any judgment in his attitude nor disapproval. He appears to accept everything I tell him as though my life is a model of convention.

I'm sorry when our lunch is finished and I have to go back to the lobby to wait for my mother.

·4·

"I'm going out," Kitty said.

Eric and I looked up.

"That's okay, Kitty. Harper and I are quite happy," he said.

She was dressed in her new voile suit we had bought that afternoon. It was fashionable and softened her work-hardened body. Her face was subtly made up to exaggerate her high cheek bones and to disguise her narrow lips. Her red hair was a shade darker and it suited. I could hardly recognize her as my mother, as the gumbooted, raincoated, windswept woman who drove the tractor and wielded the axe on Uncle Paul's farm. There was a stir of pride in me as I watched her. She seemed to feel different, too, for she no longer swore at me. Her coarse voice had vanished with her short grimy fingernails.

"May I take the car?" she asked.

"You know not to ask," said Eric. "I've told you, Kitty. Have it whenever you like."

His voice underlined *told*. It sounded slightly petulant, girlish, but Eric often sounded that way. It was his way.

"Thanks."

She moved toward the door.

"Don't keep Harper up too late," she said.

"I won't," he said.

She was dismissed. We bent over the chess board, heads almost touching. Impulsively, she came across the room and kissed me. She smelt good. Big bunches of purple violets dripping dew and nectar.

34

"Kitty's in love again," said Eric with a sigh as soon as the door had closed. "Whose turn is it?"

"Yours," I said. "Who's she in love with?"

"Ha! Got you cornered. Two more moves and it's checkmate. Some extraordinary fellow."

His hands waved, a melodramatic gesture. He tossed his head back and looked at me through lowered lids. I wasn't sure whether the look was to indicate his prowess at chess or his disapproval of the man Kitty was in love with.

"It's not that. . . ?" I could hardly pronounce the name. "That awful Thorn guy?"

"That's him. Have you moved yet?"

"No, I'm still thinking." I chewed my thumb. "Kitty's always falling in love. She's soppy."

"That's life, baby," Eric said. "You'll fall in love yourself one day."

"Not me," I said.

Eric and I always called her Kitty when we were alone—but me, never to her face. It seemed disrespectful because she was my mother and because she was so much older than me. Older than Eric, too. But we used her Christian name when we were by ourselves because it made us allies in our affection for her.

I moved a remaining castle and removed a pawn of his.

"Ha, ha," he sang. "One more move and the game's mine."

Seeing the end in sight, I lost interest.

"Eric," I said. "Who's my real father?"

He looked at me startled, eyes wide. It was a long stare and I began to feel uncomfortable. Searched around in my head for something to deflect the question but nothing materialized.

"Oh baby," he said. "You poor little kid."

He leaned over and took my face in his hands. His touch was gentle, the thumbs rubbing my cheeks.

"You mean you really don't know?" he said.

"No. She won't tell me."

35

"Well," he said.

"Tell me. I won't let on to Kitty."

"I can't," he said. "Anyway, if Kitty hasn't told you she must have a very good reason."

"What?"

I felt him shrug.

"Perhaps it's something you wouldn't understand, yet," he said.

"That's no good. I understand a lot of things. A lot more than she thinks I do."

"I believe you," he said.

"Do you think she doesn't know who it is?"

He looked at me momentarily astonished and then chortled.

"You certainly do know a lot, Harper O'Leary. I'm surprised at you."

"Do you know who it is?" I said.

He pushed me away and rose to his feet.

"Come on, baby, let's have supper."

The time was past. The bird had flown out the window, high above the room in which we sat. Too late to call it back. We went into the kitchen and made mugs of cocoa. We toasted crumpets and soaked them in golden syrup and lemon juice. The juice ran down our chins and fingers, golden streams flowing along the rivers of our veins. We looked at each other and laughed.

The swing doors opened, squeaking, jerking me from my dream. It's the man with the artificial eye.

"Still here?" he says.

"It doesn't seem very long," I say.

"I'm going to the library," he says. "Would you like to come for a walk?"

"No, I'd better not. I've got to wait for my mother."

He scratches his head, thinking.

"We could leave a message for her at the desk."

"It's okay," I say. "She'll be here any minute. Anyway, I've got lots of school work to do."

I slap my hand down on my school case too loudly, and realize that I've drawn his attention to the fact that it's closed, books firmly locked inside. The thought reaches us simultaneously. He grins.

"Sure you're happy doing all that work?" he chuckles.

I smile, blushing.

He shrugs and goes away. I know what he means. He feels sorry for me. Poor lonely child is what he really thinks.

Kitty left me many times when we were living with Eric. She didn't work. It was Thorn she was visiting and they didn't want me tagging along. She was always at the apartment when I got home from school but if she was going out before Eric arrived home, she'd say, "Be good" and "Don't go out." But she seemed preoccupied. The words were a formality. She said them because she was my mother, and they were what mothers were supposed to say.

Happy, on my own, knowing that Eric would soon be home. I'd thumb through books, neat rows of hard-backed soldiers, play the stereo, curl on the couch and watch the ant world below, one ear cocked for his key in the lock.

Excitement when I heard it. Couldn't help it. Grinning, and he grinning back. Hugs, dancing around the room. We'd topple half onto the couch, half onto the floor.

"Get off me, Harper O'Leary," he'd say. "What a way to treat a tired business man."

Giggling I'd say, "Can I get you a drink?"

Our ceremony would begin. I'd go to the cocktail cabinet, lower the sleek mahogany door, and take a crystal glass.

"Whisky?"

He'd nod.

I'd pour, tongue protruding, careful.

"Not too much," he'd say.

"Can I have one, too?"

"Lemonade for you. In the fridge."

The kitchen was pale yellow, chicken yellow, high-benched with long glass panels overlooking the city. The fridge was black. I'd open the door, take out the lemonade bottle, and pour into a fine Bohemian glass tumbler.

Back in the living room, we'd sip our drinks and Eric would ask me about my day.

"It was all right," I'd say. "Miss Crookbain was in a bad mood again. But guess what?"

He'd say that he couldn't imagine and pretend to be intrigued.

"Next year, in Mrs. McDonald's class, we're going on a trip down to a forestry camp and the limestone caves and to a dairy farm. We're going to stay at a camping ground in some cabins."

He'd look at me when I told him things like that with his teasing-serious expression.

"I suppose you'll be saving up for something expensive like that?" he'd say. "Would you like to earn some money?"

I knew immediately what it was. His shower. Leaping up I'd rush to his bathroom. He had his own off his bedroom, mottled blue tiles imported from Italy. I'd run the shower, feeling the water with my hands, waiting for the heat to come through. Then go to the linen cupboard in the hall to choose the biggest, softest towels to lay out for him.

"It's ready," I'd call.

When he was showered, he'd call, "Come on, Bluebird, come and sing to me while I cook a meal."

He often called me "Bluebird" now that I'd started going to that private school. My uniform was blue. A blue gingham dress piped in white. Our hats were blue, and our shoes. I imagined that if we could have bought them, our socks would have been blue, too. They were white. Eric paid the fees.

We'd sing, me shrill, off key, Eric sure and holding the tune. The skillet would steam blue smoke, thin slithers of meat, a touch of soya sauce, wine, garlic—Eric took pride in cooking. We'd eat in the kitchen, a bottle of wine between us, small watered down glasses for me, large for him. Mellow we'd feel at the end of it all.

"No more loitering," he'd say suddenly. "Up and away, scholar. Homework for you while I clean up in here."

He knew everything, Eric. Math, English, French—it didn't matter what I asked him, he always knew the answers. His knowledge was endless.

Mrs. Keyes is walking up and down outside the lobby, going to the front door, back this way, peering in at me. Her face is disapproving. Obsessed she is, preoccupied with our business. Thinks it's a disgrace the way I've been left. Perhaps she thinks I've been abandoned in her establishment. The thought makes me laugh inside.

It's Mrs. Carter now. I pretend not to notice as she goes over to the front door, back this way, swings the glass doors to the lobby open, pops her head in.

"Still here, love?"

I want to say, no I left ages ago. I nod.

"Mother not back yet?"

"No," I say. "It must be taking her longer than she thought."

"What's taking her such a long time, love?"

I pretend not to hear.

She clucks and goes away, no doubt to report to the proprietress.

I'll go outside. I'll wait in the street by the wall. They won't see me there and feel disturbed by my presence.

For a few seconds I wait by the swing doors, peering into the hall to see that it's empty. All clear. I rush across it, prickly down my back, scared that they'll come out and catch me—through the front door so fast that my dress catches—across the porch, down the path, down the short flight of steps that lead to the street. I huddle on the bottom step, hard against the wall. Looking back, I can see the upstairs windows but nothing of the rest of the house. I'm safe from their snooping.

People stare as they walk past. I must look strange, bunched up, knees to chin, in the shadow of the wall.

Sometimes at Eric's I'd wake to find Kitty not there. Her bed hadn't been slept in. Lying rumpled as she'd thrown them down were the clothes she'd worn the day before. Strange feeling, slightly disturbing, the void that my mother's absence created. It was like a front tooth missing or the gap which a neighboring and familiar tree would leave when it was cut down. I'd lie pondering, making up stories of weird and bizarre proportions until, made tearful by my own imagination, I'd have to go to Eric's room for reassurance.

"Kitty's not home," I'd say standing at the side of his bed, looking down at the sleeping figure, feeling no remorse at waking him. "Eric. Eric! Are you awake? Kitty's not home. She hasn't been home all night."

He'd roll over, thrashing, rubbing his eyes. He'd groan as he tried to comprehend my words. He was slow at waking, little pieces of him stretching and peeking cautiously. There was an astonishment, a slight uncomprehending quality to his waking.

"What's the time?" he'd say, blinking.

"I don't know. It's light. Kitty hasn't been home all night."

"Get in under the comforter," he'd say. "Don't stand there shivering. You look as cold as a corpse."

Wrong thing for him to have said. My body would shudder as pictures of the mutilated form of my mother, graphic, technicolor, passed through my mind.

"Do you think she'll be all right?"

"Are you worried?"

"No. Well . . . just a bit. She could've been murdered."

"Oh, Harper. You know perfectly well where she is."

"How do I know?"

He'd sigh, stretching sleepily.

"She went out with Thorn last night, didn't she?"

"Yes. But that doesn't mean she's still with him."

"Of course it does. Now stop worrying and go and make me a cup of tea."

I'd slip away careful not to sway the bed too much as I climbed off.

In the kitchen, I'd boil the kettle, cut thin slices of bread and butter them, set the tray, being careful not to forget anything. Eric was fussy about things like that. A clean tray cloth, the fine bone china and a milk jug.

I'd look out the window at the world below which was starting to wake. Often there would be people as small as miniature porcelain figures walking their dogs in the park. The plumber's truck would graunch and hiccough down the road. He always left for work at this hour. There was, occasionally, a man in shorts and T-shirt, running, huffs of hot breath streaming in front of his face. Even from that distance, I could tell he was red and sweaty.

Putting on my housecoat, I'd open the front door and catch the lift to the ground floor. Usually, I met Mrs. Thomas from the second floor. We'd nod and mutter good morning. She'd cough a deep husky cigarette cough. I'd gather the milk and the paper and catch the lift up to our apartment.

Eric had always gone back to sleep by the time I'd made the tea. I'd stand by the bed balancing the tray, nagging at him to wake up.

He'd mutter, eyes still closed.

"Hurry up or I'll drop it."

Immediately awake, he'd bounce over and pat his lap to show that that was where the tray should go. He'd make appreciative noises as I climbed onto the foot of the bed. While we drank and ate, he'd read the paper.

"What do you know," he'd say. "The government's making more money available for housing loans."

"That's neat," I'd say, not having the faintest idea what he was talking about.

I felt secure with Eric. Happy and reassured. His casual approach to Kitty's absences always comforted me, but I would rather she'd been there. I didn't really like her being away for too long. Somewhere amongst the warmth that Eric exuded, there lingered an emptiness that only my mother could fill.

We had a Christmas party. Great excitement it was, planning and preparing for it. Kitty became swept up in our enthusiasm and stayed home more often. Eric, Kitty and I went shopping together. Piled high with parcels, we'd trudge back to the car in the late evening, heap everything onto the back seat and with the three of us squeezed into the front, we'd drive home. The radio would be on.

"Si-lent night, Ho-ly night,

A-ll is calm . . ." Eric and I would sing. Kitty would hum the descant.

Eric took me shopping one day to buy Kitty's present. After much dithering and tongue chewing, I settled for a toilet bag, frilled nylon, plastic-lined, which contained a tin of talc and a cake of sweet-smelling toilet soap. Kitty and I bought Eric two leather-bound volumes of *The Life and Times of Bertrand Russell*. They meant nothing to me but the books felt smooth, shone with silver lettering, and had the smell of newly-bound paper. I was more than satisfied.

"You must buy Thorn something," Kitty said.

I said that I didn't want to.

"He'll have something for you," she said.

I bought him a ballpoint pen and a notebook. It cost me a dollar eighty.

One day Kitty and I went shopping for my first long dress. We arrived home with a navy-blue voile, shirred around the bodice and with a deep frill around the hem. It was splattered with tiny red dots. To match, I had a new pair of slightly heeled shoes. I had to try them on and parade in front of Eric and my mother.

"My goodness," Eric said, taking my hands and dancing me around the room. "You look beautiful. Just like a film star."

He and Kitty laughed and seemed delighted with me. I wished that we could stay with Eric forever. Just the three of us.

There was great activity in the kitchen as the night of the party approached. Eric and Kitty falling over each other and sometimes falling out in their efforts to fill tins, the fridge and the freezer. Countless times a day my mother would call, "Harper, run down to the dairy, dear, I've run out of butter" or "I need some more cocoa" or "Oh God! I haven't got anything for lunch. Run and get a packet of sausages. Quickly."

On the day of the party, Kitty and I made a visit to the hairdresser. I felt beautiful, with a myriad of soft curls around my face. Eric and Kitty kept telling me to leave the mirrors alone or I'd wear them out. Decorations were hung, the Christmas tree decked out, and, when everything was prepared to

43

their satisfaction, it was bathtime. I was dizzy with excitement, pins in my legs and arms, a cluster of bird flutter in my chest. Kitty painted my lips with a pale pink lipstick, and Eric pinned a pearl and gold broach to my dress.

I didn't know that Eric had so many exotic and unusual friends. I wandered among them carrying trays, revelling in the admiration I was drawing, and absorbing their clothes, their hairstyles, snippets of conversation.

"My de-e-ar. How fa-a-a-bulous!"

"You look mar-ar-vellous!"

"And he said, 'I want my John back.' Do you see? My JOHN! Ha ha ha."

They were funny people, almost as though they'd put on fancy dress for the occasion. I wondered why I'd never seen anything like them before—in the street or the shops or the pictures.

There was a woman there with her hair cut short like a man's. It was dyed green and pink, the stripes going diagonally across her skull. There were safety pins hanging from her ears. She had on a satin top with thin, thin straps and no bra. I knew because her nipples poked through. Embarrassment when I looked at her. Her friend wore white leather boots. She had a large purple rose on her dress. They must've felt shy, because they stood in the corner most of the time holding hands. Eric talked a lot to a man who'd shaved all his hair off. Maybe he'd been sick. It was just starting to grow again and looked prickly. My fingers itched everytime I went near him. With him was a dark man who had a big leather belt like a dog collar around his neck. It had a silver skull hanging from it. The skull lay on his bare chest. He didn't wear a shirt, just a gray striped jacket, and bright yellow pantaloons.

People started to dance. It was hilarious. I lounged on the

44

sofa giggling to myself. Nobody minded who they danced with. Men with men, women with women, men with women.

Eric danced with the prickly-headed guy. The did the bump and looked so funny that my tummy hurt, I laughed so much. But my mother wasn't amused.

She said, "Harper, it's nearly half-past eleven. You go off to bed now."

I pouted.

"It's too early."

"Go on," she said. "I'll come and say goodnight in a few minutes."

"Kitty, come and dance."

It was a tall, skinny man with shoe horns in his ears and a floral piece of curtain material posing as a scarf.

"Off you go," she said as he dragged her toward the music.

I climbed onto the window seat behind the Christmas tree with a glass of lemonade which I'd laced generously with gin. No one noticed me doing it. I didn't like it much. I couldn't understand why grown-ups drank it but I persevered, because I expected some miraculous propulsion into the adult world from its bitter taste.

When I woke up, the room felt cold, smelt stale. The stereo wafted nightclub music. A couple, clutching each other, moved drunkenly to the sound. The kitchen light was on and voices—slurred, bawdy, punctuated with laughter—drifted through the apartment. In the dim light, the living room looked a ghastly nightmare. Eric's beautiful carpet was splattered with broken glass and the dark stains of spilt wine. The table was littered with the remnants of supper—the remains of a jungle orgy. Ashtrays, overflowing with the smoked-out ends of cigarettes, spewed dust over the polished surfaces. I wondered where Eric and my mother were. I supposed they'd gone to bed. As I picked my way across the room, the dancers paused.

45

"Look," said the man. "The fairy's come down from the Christmas tree."

They thought this funny and doubled up laughing. I thought them stupid.

In my bedroom, I turned on the light and stood horrified. A couple were lying on my bed, the man's bare buttocks rising like rounded humps, gyrating frenetically. The woman's legs gripped his thighs, they were unaware of my intrustion. I switched the light off hastily. Flushed at what I'd seen, I rushed to Eric's room and flicked his light switch. He'd be there, I knew, curled into his sleeping position.

"Eric," I said. "There's a man and a lady on my. . . ."

I was stunned. Sent whirling into timeless confusion. Eric was in the arms of Nick, the man who wore earrings and jangling bracelets. The man who wore an embroidered kaftan and waved his arms around. He saw me over Eric's shoulder and hissed at me. Fled, out the front door, down the stairs, all the way to the ground floor.

What was happening? Where was my mother?

For a long time I sat on the bottom step unable to piece together the bizarre scenes I'd just witnessed. I didn't understand.

Some people meandered down the stairway noisily. They were from Eric's party. I took no notice of them. They disgusted me. Everything was grubby, bewildering. I had never seen men kissing like that before, and I felt frightened, cast into a world to which I didn't belong and couldn't cope with.

"What're ya doing here, lovy?" one of the men said.

He patted my head.

"I'm Father Christmas," slurred another, bending down and peering into my face so that his food-and-alcohol breath made me draw back. "What'd yer like me to bring ya?"

He swayed dangerously and caught the bannister for support. I moved up a step away from them.

"Come on you guys," said a woman and they went, linking arms and singing 'Good King Wenceslas' loudly and drunkenly.

The traffic has increased now into a steady whirr. The smell of gushing exhausts and a fine film of smog lies across the skyline. There's a sudden swelling of people on the sidewalk, too. Dour, purposeful faces. Drumbeats on asphalt.

The step has become hard and cold. No one notices me. I want to cry as I watch for my mother, trying to visualize her among the crowd. She's all I've got. Just my mother and me with our suitcases and boxes.

Things became strained after the party. Kitty blamed Eric. He blamed her.

"She's your responsibility," he said.

"What a flaming cheek," she snapped. "I'd never have left her if I'd known. . . ."

They glared at one another.

Kitty didn't say the thing that was between them, but I knew it had something to do with Nick and what I'd seen but didn't fully understand. They argued and disliked each other for it, though, and because Mrs. Thomas had found me asleep in the lobby downstairs and had let them know how disgraceful she thought it was.

It was because Nick was always at our place, too, bounding in in the evenings and staying late. And Kitty had to stay home with me because Eric and Nick began going out together. She would sit sullen, not saying much, but with that hard, determined look in her eyes. And she picked on me. She complained

47

about Nick all the time. Said he was boring. Said that she couldn't understand Eric. If he had to be like that, why couldn't he find someone more acceptable?

Her criticism made Eric angry.

"You don't have to stay," he'd say. "In fact, I'd prefer it if you didn't."

"I bet," was all Kitty said, but her eyes were resentful, her mouth set in silent disapproval. Her movements changed to stolid, almost insolent reminders of our presence, and for the first time I began to feel awkward in Eric's apartment. I felt as though we were something superfluous that he didn't know how to dispose of. But Kitty was determined to stay in spite of the strained atmosphere that wafted like a bad smell through the apartment. Sometimes I got the feeling that she expected Eric to keep us, that it was his duty.

Yet, it spite of the tension between them, his attitude toward me hadn't changed. The time we spent together was still as though we were tumbling on clouds.

Toward Kitty, he was polite but distant.

One day, Eric said that Nick was coming to live because he had nowhere to go. Kitty said that he couldn't, that she wasn't going to live with a person like that, that the whole idea was sordid. Eric said that he'd have whomever he liked in his own home.

And so, it was time to leave.

They swapped a few harsh words before we left. I cried, not so they could see, but in the bathroom where I could hear what they were saying.

Kitty called Eric a lot of swear words and said that he had no sense of obligation or responsibility. She never wanted to see him or his fruity friends again she said. He was a disgusting corruption of a human being.

I couldn't understand why she was being so nasty. We'd only

been invited to stay a few days and we'd stayed for months and months. Eric had been good to us. Nick wasn't so bad. I wouldn't mind having him live in the place. But she was through with it all.

Eric retaliated. He called her a red-headed bitch, a grasping old hag, a cheap harlot.

In a way, I was glad to be getting out of the place. They hated each other.

We went to live with Thorn.

"Hello, young lady."

It's Mr. Wilson, the man with the artificial eye. Didn't see him approaching but he's standing above me, his arms full of library books.

"Aren't you cold?" he says.

He doesn't say, 'Still waiting for your mother?' I'm grateful for that.

"Not really," I say.

"Come on inside anyway," he says. "You can't sit here all night."

"I think I'll wait for a bit longer," I say. "It's quite nice here."

He looks down at me. Ponders. One shrewd eye.

"Come on. She'll be back just as quickly, whether you're inside or out."

We got into the boarding house together.

"Up you go and get something warm to put on," he says. "I'll wait for you in the lobby and then we'll have a bite to eat. I'm hungry, aren't you?"

· 5 ·

They've made me feel different, these women in the boarding house, watching me all day, whispering about my clothes and my circumstances. I'm anxious, too. My mother should be back. After dinner I'll ring the police. They're the only people I can think of, we know so few. Perhaps she went to Thorn's to collect the rest of our belongings and he's murdered her. Perhaps she's been run over or had a heart attack in a taxi. No one would know about me. I'd be an orphan.

I visualize a square stone building, cold and formidable, with ivy clinging to the bars over the windows. Read a story about such a place once, in a book which belonged to my grandmother when she was my age. I'm dressed in brown serge like all the other girls, am pale, undernourished with thin red welts spiralling up my legs where the bitter-faced mistresses have lashed me. At night, as I lie under the one gray blanket on my hard narrow bed, I cry and plan how to escape. Then one day, as I'm lingering by the iron gates, Eric goes past. He sees me and takes me away with one of the little girls, my favorite, called Roseanna. We live with him in an apartment high over the city. . . .

"Would you like soup?"

Mr. Wilson's voice cuts across my daydream.

"No, thank you. I don't like soup very much."

"I think I'll give it a miss, too," he says. "What about the roast mutton? That's what I'm going to have."

I study the menu, a spotted square of cardboard.

"I'll have that, too," I say.

He orders and Mrs. Carter goes away toward the kitchen.

"I was born on a train," I say proudly.

I need to talk. About myself. To tell Mr. Wilson the extraordinary events of my life in the hope that, somewhere among them, I'll find a thread of normality, something to make me like all the other girls of my age. I want to be reassured that it's a common thing for girls of my age to be left in boarding houses all day.

He leans back in his chair and says, "Go on. Well, I never. How did that happen?"

"My mother was going home to her mother but I couldn't wait until she got there."

"Fancy that," he says. "How's your mutton?"

"It's all right. My mother says I've always been too impatient. Started off that way and been like it ever since, she says."

"You've been a very patient young lady today," he says.

"Oh that's different. It's only some things I'm impatient about. Like school projects and exams and that sort of thing. And being born of course."

It's a joke and I laugh loudly. He chuckles politely with me.

"She was living in Roxton when she was expecting me and she wanted to go to my grandmother in Kawangai. We don't like my grandmother because she wasn't very nice to us when we lived with her. Anyway, there were all these people on the train. Lots of soldiers and skiers and people like that. It was winter, you see. My birthday's at the end of May."

"In May eh?" says Mr. Wilson. "I wonder how old you'll be next May?"

I refuse to be distracted.

"It was cold, my mother said. You know, rain in Roxton when they left, fog all the way across Dairy Flats with cows

51

looking like black ghosts, snow crippling the center of the island. But she said that it was nice and warm in the train. They had central heating and everyone had rugs and railway-issue pillows. It seemed as though it was going to be a good journey, or so she thought. At Olivetown, they all rushed onto the platform for cups of tea and ham sandwiches and guess what happened?"

"I can't imagine," he says. "Why don't you eat your dinner?"

I take a mouthful of the cooling roast mutton.

"She started to have contractions."

I watch his face for reaction—surprise, disapproval, embarrassment. Nothing. He looks at me politely and eats steadily as though I were describing a flower show. Disappointment.

"I was on my way," I continue, still scrutinizing his face which remains flat. "They weren't very regular at first—the—the—contractions—so she didn't worry, but they became more and more frequent. She was timing them with her watch, you see. And then, you wouldn't believe it! The water bag burst. That's the sort of bag like plastic that. . . ."

I'm enjoying myself. The day has made me angry and aggressive. I don't care that I may shock Mr. Wilson, or anyone else for that matter. I'd like to say something really rude to the woman who runs this establishment, but I can't get at her. So, Mr. Wilson will do.

"She was lucky," I say, "because she was near the Ladies' Room, so she rushed in there and locked the door. She stayed there for ages, she said, feeling pretty rotten and frightened. But, after a while, she felt better so she went back to her seat, and the next thing, the contractions were starting all over again. I think that's the way it went."

"That sounds about right," he says.

Swept away by the power of my own story, I ignore the touch of weariness in his voice.

"And then next," I say slowly, trying to piece together the

sequence of events as I'd heard them, "she had this awful pain in her back and, all of a sudden, she vomited all over herself and the lady sitting next to her. She said that she felt just terrible. The lady was angry to start with, until my mother told her what was wrong. Then she panicked and pulled the emergency cord. The train stopped. Clanked and groaned and skidded down the lines and stopped. Dead. Right in the middle of all that ice and snow."

I pause so that the drama of the occasion sinks in. Mr. Wilson raises an eyebrow and whistles softly. Imagining him to be impressed, I go on.

"My mother said that the lady got off the train and ran up and down yelling. Other people got off, too, and there was terrible confusion because most people didn't know why the train had stopped. They thought there'd been an accident. Someone shouted out for a doctor but there wasn't one. Then this guard came, you see, and rigged up a rug to shield my mother and he shooed everyone out of the carriage. He was kind, my mother said, and told her what to do. He said that he'd been present at the births of all his six children so he knew all about it. Imagine! Six children."

I feel that my efforts at being grown up are misfiring, but Mr. Wilson helps me out.

"You seem to know a great deal about it," he says. "I'd almost believe you were there."

I laugh. High-pitched laughter tinged with hysteria.

"I've heard my mother tell it so many times," I say. "She tells everyone. It's her favorite story. I can recite it off by heart now." I poke at the baked potato which reminds me of waterlogged skin. "I did see a film once about a baby being born. That's how I know."

"I see," he says. "How about dessert? Would you like peaches and ice cream or apple pie?"

I think for a moment.

"Peaches and ice cream'll do," I say.

He gives the order.

"Do you want to hear what happened next?" I say.

"Now that you've told me so much you may as well finish," he says.

He's quite pleasant about it and it's all the encouragement I need.

"The guard told my mother that an ambulance had been called and it would be waiting for us at Ratahine. Then I was born." I smile at him proudly. "I squawked like a hungry bird, my mother said. She said that the guard wrapped me in a nightgown of hers and held me up at the window for everyone to see. They all cheered. My mother said that she felt sad that the first breath her little baby took was full of soot and cigarette smoke and the smell of oranges. It didn't worry me though."

Our dessert arrives and we eat in silence. I feel deflated. A little foolish.

"And was the ambulance there?" Mr. Wilson asks.

He's aware of my embarrassment.

"Yes. We went to Ratahine hospital."

"So it all ended well." He's smiling. Kindly. "You certainly had an unusual beginning young lady. And it's an unusual name—Harper."

"The guard who helped my mother was Mr. Harper. I was named after him."

I feel none of the usual pride in announcing this. My mood has changed. Subdued. My anxiety becomes more acute.

"Excuse me," I say. "I must see if my mother's back yet. She won't know where I am."

He doesn't try to stop me but pats my arm. A sympathetic gesture.

·6·

She's there, in the entrance hall. So are Mrs. Keyes and Mrs. Carter. I rush to my mother, relief flowing through me.

"You're back at last," I say.

"She is, child," says Mrs. Keyes.

Her voice, vibrating around the walls, loudly proclaims her disapproval. She looks enormous in the weak half-light that umbrellas down from the ceiling. Her arms rest on cushion breasts and her dark face glowers so that I hesitate half-way to my mother, looking from one to the other. There's tension in the air. My mother looks wild. Storm-tossed. I move close to her. Her hair sweeps upward from her face. Her eyes are red-rimmed, the pupils dilated. Dark smudges brush her cheek bones. She's been crying.

"What's the matter? What's going on?" I say.

"Nothing, honey," she says, putting an arm around me and squeezing.

She's pleased to see me.

"To continue our discussion since you brought the subject up in the first place," Mrs. Keyes says coldly to my mother, "this is hardly the place to leave a child while you go gallivanting off for the day."

My mother's body stiffens but she makes no reply.

"You had no right to leave her here," Mrs. Keyes goes on. "I hadn't the time to look after her and neither had my staff."

Mrs. Carter nods agreement.

"It's a disgrace," she says. "No one to stop her reading those filthy sex magazines."

"What sex magazines?" says my mother. "Anyway, it's none of your business what my daughter reads."

They gasp. Together. Like a chorus.

"Anything could have happened to her." Mrs. Keyes looks so stern that I want to laugh, but I control it because we're involved in the serious matter of reprimanding my mother. I keep my face passive and she continues to reproach us. "At one point, I nearly called the police. Do you realize that your child disappeared for almost three hours?"

"The police?" My mother nearly chokes.

"I was outside," I say. "On the steps."

No one takes any notice of me.

"I was all right," I say louder, my voice strangely high-pitched.

My mother turns on me.

"Where were you, Harper?" she says. "What've you been doing? Can't I leave you by yourself for a day without something going wrong?"

It's awful. I could die. Why does she have to make a scene in front of everyone?

"I told you, I was out on the steps."

"There you are," says my mother looking at the two women triumphantly.

"We still had to keep on eye on her," says Mrs. Carter, standing behind the bulk of the proprietress which gives her cover and confidence. "It did interrupt our work."

"What the hell are you talking about?" says mother defensively. "Harper's quite capable of looking after herself for a day. She doesn't need self-appointed babysitters."

"Really," says Mrs. Keyes snootily. "There's no need for that sort of talk. And I would be pleased, Mrs. . . . Mrs. . . . ."

"O'Leary," snaps my mother.

"Yes. I would be pleased if this child wasn't left to her own devices again. Come along, Mrs. Carter."

"Just a minute," shouts my mother so loudly that I expect everyone to come rushing out of the dining room. "I won't stand here and be insulted like that."

Mrs. Keyes turns around. She's angry now. I wish I could tiptoe away and hide. My mother's so embarrassing.

"Insults, Mrs. O'Leary?" Mrs. Keyes says, her voice controlled and precise. "You neglect your daughter all day and then you stand in my hallway and shout my house down. How dare you! If you can't control yourself, I'll have to ask you to leave. I can't have my guests disturbed by your disgusting behavior."

"Disgusting," shrieks my mother, the trigger of self-control suddenly snapping. "You old bitch. You insult me and my daughter. . . ."

"Stop that language in my house," booms Mrs. Keyes. "I won't have it."

They're shouting now, all together, not listening to what anyone else is saying. It's like fireworks. Bang after bang ricocheting off the walls. Clatter and smoke. Streamers of insults strangling each other in a great holocaust of rage. I feel hot. Prickly all over as though I've eaten gooseberries and come out in hives. Rings of welts burn my skin. I want to tear my flesh, strip it from my body, and drown in iced water.

"You're a pack of moralizing, narrow-minded, screwed-up, fucking bitches," my mother screams.

Her face is ugly with defiance, guilt and rage. I've never felt so ashamed.

"Listen to you. And you call yourself a mother," shrills Mrs. Carter.

"You barren bag," my mother yells, turning on her. "What the hell do you know about it?"

57

"Stop it. Stop it at once," booms Mrs. Keyes, "or I'll call the police."

"You call the police and see what happens to you."

My mother takes a threatening step toward Mrs. Keyes, and I'm afraid she'll smash her fist into the woman's face. I grab her wrists but she shakes me off. My gesture seems to penetrate her rage because she straightens up and her arms fall to her sides. Mrs. Keyes has simmered down a little, too. She looks enormous and remote. Like a large and distant mountain.

"I want you out of this house now, Mrs. O'Leary," she says. "Now. With your daughter and your luggage."

She kicks her foot at our big tin trunk which I hadn't noticed before. My mother must have brought it from Thorn's.

"Oh no," my mother laughs bitterly. "I've paid for tonight and we're staying."

"I'll gladly give you a refund," says Mrs. Keyes and walks toward the desk.

I'm paralyzed. With fear. We'll be cast into the street, again, luggage and all, with nowhere to go. The same thought occurs to my mother, for she backs down a little.

"Look," she says. "You can't do that. We've got nowhere . . . I mean, Harper's tired. All this shifting around isn't good. . . ."

"You should have thought of that before," says Mrs. Keyes.

No one moves. The proprietress's face is purple and she breathes heavily. Her forehead is damp. Mrs. Carter is pale but still excited. My mother is guilty and upset. In the sudden hushed light, the figures look like distorted wax models. There's a soft hum from the traffic outside and the wind gives an eerie quality to the evening. The stillness inside is suffocating, more frightening than the explosion of uncontrolled rage which rampaged around a few moments ago. No one wants to give in first. It's fleeting. A couple of heart beats, but it seems to go on forever. I want to throw myself at my mother for protection. Instead, I cough and shuffle my feet.

"Very well," says Mrs. Keyes wearily. "But you'll be out first thing in the morning. You haven't paid for breakfast, and there'll be none for you."

I stand, dumb. I wish my mother would say thank you to Mrs. Keyes, would show some gratitude, but she bends to pick up the trunk, without a word.

"Here let me."

It's Mr. Wilson. He bends to take the trunk from my mother and, as he does so, I scrutinize his face for reaction. Which side will he be on?

"Harper can manage," snaps my mother and my insides freeze again at her rudeness. He doesn't seem to notice. In fact, from the look on his face, he seems to find my mother quite attractive. To me she looks ugly and I wish she wasn't my mother.

"Don't bother, Mr. Wilson," says Mrs. Keyes. "It's a waste of time. We've looked after her child all day and you should've heard the abuse."

"I did," he says lifting the trunk anyway. "Harper's hardly a child, though. She's quite a young lady in fact."

He grins at my mother who looks slightly taken aback. I guess she didn't expect anyone to say nice things about me in this establishment.

"Do what you like then," says Mrs. Keyes. "Come along, Mrs. Carter. Our guests have been upset enough by that woman's outburst."

She turns and goes toward the dining room. I want to call out that I'm sorry. I hate my mother to make people so angry.

"Come on," says Mr. Wilson. "I'll help you up the stairs."

His voice is friendly and contains a soothing quality that jerks me away from the paralyzing involvement of adult conflict.

"Thank you," says my mother meekly.

She's hanging on tightly to her voice which wobbles. Tossing her hair back she takes a couple of deep breaths and stoops toward the handle of the trunk. We trudge up the stairs. No one speaks until we're in our room.

"I'm sorry," Mr. Wilson says. "That sort of thing is most unpleasant."

My mother shrugs.

"I'm sure it'll have blown over by morning," he says, making no move to leave.

"Thank you for your help," says my mother, dismissing him.

He looks directly at her. It's a funny, appreciative look.

"I wish I could've done more. Good night. Good night, Harper."

He goes quietly, shutting the door.

Now that he's gone, I cry. My mother hugs me saying, "Don't cry. Don't cry, Harper. Everything'll be all right, love." And she cries, too. Suddenly, we're laughing. Laughing and crying and hugging each other. Because we're both upset.

"Here, silly, wash your face," she says, at last, pulling away from me.

Running water into the basin, she douses her face. I do the same and feel comforted by the coarse rub of the towel on my cheeks. My mother flings off her shoes and throws herself onto the bed.

"Where'd you go?" I say.

"All over the place."

"You've been to Thorn's haven't you?"

"Only to get the rest of our things."

"Was he awful to you?"

"A bit. You know Thorn."

"What'd he say?"

"Harper, I'm tired, dear."

She closes her eyes.

"Did you find somewhere for us to live?"

"I think so," she says, eyes still shut. "It'll be okay. You mustn't worry. I'm going to be a housekeeper for a rich old lady."

I want to say that that'll be a change from living with men but I don't. I toy with the things on the dressing table, pushing the brush around like a car, making a road out of the fine film of dust.

"What's it like?" I say.

She doesn't answer.

"What's the place like?" I say again.

"Quite nice. We've got a little house out the back all to ourselves. You'll see tomorrow."

"What's the lady like?"

"Harper, I'm exhausted. Why don't you go and have a bath. You haven't had one since Tuesday."

The thought of a bath terrifies me. I'd have to leave the safety of our room and go down the corridor to the bathroom. There mightn't be a lock on the bathroom door.

There's a knock.

I jump.

"Oh hell," says my mother.

She sits up, brushing the hair off her face, pushing her feet into her shoes, rallying her resources in preparation for another confrontation.

"See who it is," she says.

I stare at her open mouthed, petrified.

"Open it," she says.

There's another knock, more persistent this time and then I hear Mr. Wilson's voice. I rush to open the door.

"We thought it was Mrs. Keyes," I say grinning relief, standing back to let him in.

61

"Sorry if I startled you." He looks beyond me to my mother. "I thought you might appreciate a cup of tea."

He's carrying a tray with tea things on it and I think, as he pushes aside the remains of my racing car circuit and puts it down on the dressing table, that it's like the good fairy arriving.

"That's marvelous," says my mother. "How on earth did you manage it?"

He chuckles.

"I've been staying here for a number of years now. It's given me a free pass into the inner sanctuary. I'm trusted to help myself to tea and biscuits from the kitchen whenever I like. So." He looks at my mother as though she's beautiful. "Here it is."

My mother laughs.

"It's not going to make you very popular with the management."

"Don't you worry about that," says Mr. Wilson. "I can take care of myself."

Suddenly my mother's head is bent and her shoulders shake in silent sobs. The day has been so wretched for her that this act of kindness seems to have overwhelmed her. Mr. Wilson pats her shoulder.

"There now," he says. "There now."

I suppose he can't think of anything else to say. He stands awkwardly looking down at her. I don't like Mr. Wilson seeing my mother cry.

"How about pouring the tea, Harper?" he says, noting my embarrassment.

I'm pleased to have something to do.

"I'm sorry," says my mother but she doesn't stop. I suppose she can't.

"Have a good cry," he says. "You'll feel better."

She snuffles and blows her nose. It sounds rude. I search Mr.

Wilson's face for signs of disgust, but his expression is sympathetic.

"Here's your tea," I say, handing her a cup.

"Thanks, dear."

She keeps her head bowed.

"Mr. Wilson?"

"No, that's for you," he says. "I only brought two cups up. It's a bit early for me."

I perch on the corner of my bed and he sits beside me.

"This's an awful place to stay in," I say, trying to distract him from my crying mother.

"It's certainly not the best in the world, is it?" he says, twinkling, helping me. "But it's handy to everything I want to do when I'm in Roxton."

"Don't you live here all the time, then?" I say, a clutch of panic in my chest. I had taken it for granted that Mr. Wilson was one of the permanents, and would be available to act as a buffer should we need one.

"No," he says. "I come down here about once a year for a bit of a rest and to do business. But I'm only forty miles away. At Ngaurimu. Do you know where that is?"

I shake my head.

My mother gets up and goes to the dressing table. Even from side-on her eyes look swollen. She pats them with the face cloth.

"It's north of here. On the west coast. Just a village. You wouldn't have heard of it," Mr. Wilson says.

"I'd like to go there. It sounds nice," I say, too eagerly.

He laughs.

"You'd be most welcome," he says.

My mother, having recovered at last, says, "I'm terribly sorry. I've had an upsetting day."

"Don't worry about it," Mr. Wilson says. "We all have those

63

days sometimes. Actually, Harper and I had quite a pleasant day—off and on. She's told me a lot about herself."

He looks over my head at my mother, that adult look which says, 'I understand. She's told me far more than she realizes and I'm aware of your predicament.'

I watch them, feeling resentful. Mr. Wilson's my friend. My discovery, and already they have some sort of understanding that excludes me. But it's transitory. He turns to me.

"Harper wants me to get a pink eye. Don't you?"

"A pink and white striped one."

We laugh.

My mother looks puzzled. This is our private joke which excludes her.

"Anyway," says Mr. Wilson, "I must be getting along. I've got some letters to write and you must be feeling tired."

It's my mother again.

He takes a pencil and a notebook from his pocket and tears a page out. Leaning it against the wardrobe door, he writes.

"Now, I don't want you to be offended or to think that I'm compromising you in any way," he says, "but I want you to take my address. I only have a small house with one spare room, but I'd love you and Harper to come and stay with me. Anytime . . . sometime . . . if you need. . . ." He shrugs. My mother looks amazed. "It's a genuine offer. I'm quite sincere. You'd both be more than welcome . . . here."

The paper flutters as he holds it out.

I'm too stunned, too delighted to move. Then a quick rush of anger sweeps over me as I notice my mother's face. It's surprise and a reluctance to accept. I reach over and snatch the paper before he changes his mind.

"That's very kind of you but . . ." she says.

"I know," he says, holding up his hand. "You can't accept

addresses from strange men. But look on me as a friend. Your daughter does."

She smiles slightly and says, "Thank you."

"Good," he says. "We'll see each other again sometime. Now don't you lose that paper, Harper."

When he's gone, I dance around the room.

"It's all fixed up. We'll go and live with Mr. Wilson at Ngaurimu. Isn't he nice?"

My mother says, "No. We won't."

I can hardly believe my ears. I don't understand her.

"Why? Why not? He asked us."

"Because we don't accept . . . accept . . . charity," she says. "We're going to housekeep for Mrs. Eagles."

I flounce.

Sulk.

I'll never understand grownups.

·7·

I wait with our luggage outside a small lean-to cottage in the backyard while my mother goes into the big house to see Mrs. Eagles. The cottage, though neat, is a far cry from the remote splendor of Mrs. Eagles's home, with its Tudor-style exterior and gabled windows. From the long gravel driveway, it looks like one of those expensive country manors with manicured lawns and sharp-edged flower beds. Even the trees, although not pruned to a tidiness which makes them look unnatural, are trimmed to indicate that any unruly growth is vigorously controlled. I wonder who is responsible. I can't imagine an old lady coping with this huge garden. But then, if she's rich, she'll probably have a gardener.

The humidity today is killing and the leaves droop like scraps of fabric—expensive fabric, within the confines of the high brick walls surrounding the section. The gates are high, too. Iron bars bent into curls and squiggles.

Good for swinging on, I think.

My dress is sticking to my back. I sit in the shade under an apple tree and feel the prick of dried grass, sharp as a new-mown hay paddock, on the backs of my legs. There's a stillness in this garden as though we're cut off from people and cars and city noises. Even the wind seems to have bypassed us. A solitary blackbird hops across the lawn in front of me and he too looks sun-faded and exhausted.

Wish my mother would hurry. I get sick of waiting for her.

The heat makes me drowsy. I close my eyes and wonder what Mrs. Eagles will be like. I've never really known an old person except my grandmother, and I can't remember her clearly. There were odd things, such as her purple-red hands with the wart on the joint of one of her fingers, the scrumptious cakes she used to make, and the bowls coated with mixture that I used to scrape, her frizzy hair and tired eyes. But I don't have a complete picture of her. Perhaps Mrs. Eagles will be like the wizened, toothless old lady with the shrunken jaw and hooked nose who used to travel on the same bus as me every morning. I can't imagine that old lady in the big house, though. She would suit our cottage far better.

My mother comes out waving a key.

"Here it is," she calls excitedly. "The key to our very own home, and we've got the whole afternoon to settle in. I don't have to start work until tomorrow."

The key scrapes in the lock. It's stiff.

"Come on. Come on," murmurs my mother impatiently.

And then the door is open.

"You first," she says, standing back.

"No, you," I say, momentarily apprehensive.

So we tumble in together, not knowing where to look first. It's the first real house we've ever had to ourselves, and we're both bubbling, grinning, saying incoherent things.

It's small with no kitchen but already I'm in love with it. The bedroom has two beds, with a table in between, and lace curtains at the windows. The other room is the living room with easy chairs and an electric heater. In one corner is the dining table. I inspect the cupboards and call my mother to look at the electric hotplate, hot-water kettle and toaster.

"Good," she says. "A fold-away kitchen. That'll be so that we can cook our own breakfasts and snacks."

"Is that all we're going to live on?" I say.

"Of course not," she laughs. "I'll bring you a scrumptious *cordon bleu* dinner over from the big house every night."

"Yummy," I say, rubbing my stomach and licking my lips.

She gives me a playful slap on the behind and laughs.

"Come and see what's out here."

I follow her onto a closed-in porch where there's an enormous old fashioned fridge, and through another door into the bathroom. I feel it's the most beautiful home in the world as I turn on the taps and let the cold water rush over my hands and arms.

"What do you think? Do you like it?" my mother asks anxiously.

"It's great! Just terrific," I say.

"Worth the awful day in the boarding house?"

"Sure is."

Satisfied, she goes into the living room and begins unpacking.

"Let's not do that yet," I say. "I'm starving. Let's go and buy some food and then I can try out our mini-kitchen."

"Okay ma'am," she says. "Anything you say."

The shops aren't far away. Just around a corner and across a small park. They're a typical suburban block—supermarket, dairy, butcher, a fruit store and a post office—all we need. While my mother is in the supermarket, I go into the dairy and spend the last of my pocket money on two boysenberry-flavored ice creams. The big size. The heat makes them dribble and I stand on the sidewalk, waiting, licking one and then the other. The man from the butcher shop goes past.

"Whoo-hoo," he whistles. "Those'll make you fat."

I grin at him and think that I'm going to like living in this place.

Armed with bulging paper bags, we cross the park toward our home, my mother giggling with me like one of my school friends. She's completely unconcerned by the stares and smiles we're attracting from passers by.

We sit on the steps in the sun and eat our lunch. She tells me about Mrs. Eagles. She says that because Mrs. Eagles is old she'll have some old-fashioned ideas, and that I must be careful not to upset her in any way. She says that I'm not to play on the lawns at the front of the house, never to pick anything from the garden, and never to go inside the big house.

"What if I want you for something?"

"You'll have to knock on the back door. I won't be far away," my mother says.

"What's the use of lawns if you can't play on them?"

"You can play round here," says my mother.

"There's hardly any room," I say, mentally measuring the five-meter strip at the front of our cottage.

"You'll manage," she says lightly and goes inside.

In the bathroom, I rinse the dishes in the basin and then put them away in the cupboard in the living room. My mother has hung pictures, our books are on the shelf and the room looks very much ours. She's gathering the washing.

On our way to do the laundry in the big house, she points out the various rooms.

"That's the kitchen door. Those French doors go into the dining room. Strictly out-of-bounds to you."

I look at the French doors, firmly closed, heavy moss-green curtains blocking out the sunlight and note that they have a gloomy look which reminds me of the wild arum lily leaves growing in old cemeteries. I look upwards at the second-story windows. Old Venetian blinds enfold the secrets of each room. There's something mysterious about the closed-in look which makes me shiver deliciously at the thought of ghosts.

Contented we are in the laundry, my mother washing and

spinning, me rinsing. We talk about the new school I'm to go to, and the things we'll do on her days off. The nightmarish boarding house and Thorn seem a long way behind us. It's difficult to believe that they were recently a part of my life.

Later in that afternoon a buzzer rings above our front door.

"That'll be Mrs. Eagles," says my mother.

She gets up quickly and straightens her hair, smooths the front of her dress saying, "Do I look all right? Will I do, do you think?"

She's nervous.

A few minutes later she's back, flushed, shiny-eyed.

"Go and change your dress. Quickly! Mrs. Eagles wants to meet you."

I scurry into the bedroom, pull one dress off, another one on, wiggle my feet into my good shoes, the ones with the ribbons that tie over the instep, brush my hair.

I'm nervous, too.

We enter the big house through the kitchen, which is empty and smells of detergent. It's dim and has a sterilized appearance. Following my mother down the hall, I'm aware of the many pictures hanging in heavy wooden and gilt frames. They're scenes of hills with smokey skies, ovals with sepia ladies dangling roses, roaring stags that stand in cold mountain lakes. Beyond a brown velvet curtain, we come to the drawing room door.

I've never seen a room like it except in films. It's enormous and crowded with upholstered furniture, dark sideboards and tables of solid, carved wood. Heavy drapes fall to the floor.

In a winged armchair is Mrs. Eagles. She's nothing like what I pictured her. Reminds me of a pale, shaggy dog—old and matted. She's a big woman, I can tell, even though she's sitting down, because she fills the whole chair and seems to flow over the sides. Her hair isn't gray-white and thin but bushy and an apricot color. I imagine it's dyed. Her eyes bulge as she peers at us.

"I've brought Harper, Mrs. Eagles," says my mother standing just inside the door.

"So I see," says Mrs. Eagles. "Come closer, Harper, so that I can look at you."

I move to the middle of the room feeling as wooden as her pieces of furniture. She scrutinizes me and, although I try not to stare back, I can't help noticing that her face has a lot of powder on it. It's the color of wine biscuits and looks cracked. I feel uncomfortable under her gaze but am too scared to move.

"So you are Harper," she says at last and smiles.

"Yes," says my mother, nudging me, indicating with her eyes that I'm to say something.

"How do you do," I say, feeling my cheeks burning.

"Would you like a candy?" she says and fumbles in a knitting bag on the table beside her chair. She holds out a crumpled paper bag and I plunge my hand in. Jelly beans! I can hardly believe it.

"I hope you like them," she says. "I'm fond of them."

"Thank you," I say and put the candy into my mouth.

She pops one into her mouth, crushes the top of the paper bag, and puts it back into the knitting bag. My mother misses out.

"Is she a good child?" Mrs. Eagles says to my mother.

"Very," says my mother. Her voice stiff, slightly offended.

"We will see. Have you told her not to play on the lawn?"

"Yes," says my mother.

While they're discussing me, I study the carpet and think that the browny-beige swirls are like the mud flats at the outer reaches of the harbor. I imagine crabs scuttling out of the darker brown rings which are really the centers of a faded leaf pattern.

71

"I hope she does what she is told," says Mrs. Eagles. "Children are disobedient these days, I find."

Her voice is querulous. Perhaps she doesn't approve of me.

"Mrs. O'Leary, I wish you to purchase two smocks for work," she says, and I'm relieved that she's momentarily forgotten about me. "You may buy them at Ashton and Walls. They can go on my account. I will make the necessary arrangements."

My mother says that she will and then there's silence. Mrs. Eagles is looking at me again as though she's searching for something to say. I wish I could help her out but I don't know how to. There's a tightness in my chest and I'd like the interview to be over.

"You are thin," she says finally.

"It's because I'm growing," I say.

"Speak up. I cannot hear you. I hope you are not one of those children who mumble."

I repeat myself. Loudly. Embarrassed.

"I see," she says and smiles weakly.

Another pause.

"Do you go to church? I hope so. Young people do not seem to any more."

I don't know what to say. My eyes are glued to my feet. The last time I went to church was when we lived with the Presbyterian minister. I was little and only remember it vaguely. My memory discharges visions of a partially naked man nailed to a cross, torn flesh where the nails penetrated, drops of blood and agony. I see a purple heart, light shining from its center, and a man with leprosy leaping from a tree into a crowd of people. I'm not sure. Perhaps he was blind or dead. The stories are jumbled in my head.

She's tired of waiting for my reply. She probably thinks I'm inarticulate and stupid. It's how I feel at the moment.

"It is my bridge afternoon tomorrow, Mrs. O'Leary. I will be

72

pleased if you will drive me there at one-thirty, directly after lunch."

"Yes, of course, Mrs. Eagles," says my mother.

She sounds meek. Not a bit like my mother.

They talk for a while about her other duties. I stand as petrified as the garlanded porcelain shephered by the window, praying for the agonizing meeting to be over. My whole attention is focused on him, and I'm afraid that when it's time to go I won't be able to move.

"That will be all," says Mrs. Eagles. "Oh, Mrs. O'Leary, would you please change the television to the other channel. I enjoy watching the golf. So colorful."

My mother bounds across the room and makes the necessary adjustment.

"Thank you for your time," Mrs. Eagles says and her hand plunges into the knitting bag.

We're dismissed.

I mutter goodbye but she doesn't hear me. Bob Charles has hit into a bunker.

·8·

I t's Sunday. A hazy morning, heavy with humidity and heat. We're taking Mrs. Eagles to church. I said to my mother that I didn't believe in God and didn't want to go.

"If you don't believe in God, you'd better come so that you know what you're talking about," she said.

I humphed around, snorting and muttering that it was a load of crap, but I'm going. She insisted.

I hold the car door open, watching them coming across the back veranda. This way's easier for Mrs. Eagles than going out the front. There aren't so many steps.

She's ginger colored. Leans heavily on my mother, unsteady, and a little afraid of falling, taking ages to come down the steps, so that my mother is straining under her weight. They shuffle along the path and I can see my mother's lips moving, uttering reassuring words. Mrs. Eagles's stockings are thick gray and I wonder where on earth she bought them. A black shiny material, her dress, huge and shapeless with clusters of pink and orange flowers. It makes her look like one of those ponderous floats in the Lions' Club Christmas Parade. She stumbles, and they pause until she's composed enough to go on. She has a silk shawl around her shoulders, gingery like her hair and skin. I wonder whether she's forgotten her hat or whether she doesn't wear one any more.

"Thank you, Harper," she says as she falls rather heavily into the front seat.

74

I close the door and climb into the back.

It's a long time since I've been to church and I wonder what it will be like. Reverend Wilkins, the Presbyterian minister we used to live with, insisted that my mother take me. We always sat at the back in case I made a disturbance and had to be rushed outside. Was only a little kid then—not even old enough to go to school.

He was a strange man, the Reverend Wilkins. Pale and thin and always washing his hands. He had a faraway look on his face, and most times he didn't notice me or, for that matter, anything else around him. He must have been a good man, though, because he used to say long prayers every meal time so that we always ate cool food.

Mrs. Wilkins was different. She was huge and noisy. Smelt. Dirty smell as though she never changed her underwear. But she liked me and as long as I screwed my nose up tight when she tossed me in the air and tickled my tummy, it wasn't too bad. But then, when I chuckled and sometimes screamed with laughter or excitement, she'd become alarmed and shush me up at once because the Wilkinses didn't like noise.

A quiet house, theirs. Hushed. Still, without so much as a sweep from the wind to create the slightest ripple. Dim, too, with the windows closed and the blinds drawn to keep outside noises at bay. We all moved like Chinese people, short shuffles so as not to disturb the silence. It seemed that we were pretending to have a sleeping baby or an ill grandmother in the house. I tiptoed as often as I could remember but it wasn't enough for the Wilkinses. They were always at me about noise. Kindly but firmly, they'd tell me that little girls must learn to move on padded feet like angels.

One day, I told the Reverend Wilkins that there didn't seem to be much angel in me. "Keep trying," he said. "God always rewards a trier."

My mother's face would screw up with anger when they remonstrated with me. Said it was unfair to expect adult behavior from a child. But to please them, she nagged at me anyway.

And, of course, there was my voice. It didn't seem loud to me but apparently it boomed in everyone else's ears. Difficult it was. If I whispered as they did, no one heard me. If I spoke normally, I was considered to be shouting and would be sent outside or into my bedroom. If I shouted, which I did sometimes to attract attention, I was whacked for deliberately disturbing the Wilkins.

Often, even on cold winter days, my mother would send me to the back of the section to play. Muttered about it though. Said it was absurd to expect a child to spend its days behaving like an old pampered cat, moving from one source of heat to another just to sleep. Children had to have somewhere to let off steam, she'd grumble as she buttoned my jacket and tied a woolen hat under my chin. The Wilkinses needed a few rowdy boys, she said. That'd swiftly change their attitude. I waited daily for those boys to arrive.

About that time, I began having nightmares. Not quiet ones where one perspires in silent panic but those full-blooded lusty ones. At night, too. When the silence was at its full strength. My voice hollered, clattering hoofs across the sacred rest time. It was too much for the Wilkinses. In the nicest possible way, they suggested that my mother should start looking around for a more suitable place to live. She must take her time, they said. Find somewhere where she would be happy and where I'd be appreciated.

One day we got into a taxi with our luggage and, after waves and goodbyes with the Wilkinses, we drove away. As we took off my mother gave an enormous sigh. Relief, I imagine Mrs.

Wilkins gave one, too. We never went back, not even for a visit, and we never went to church again. Until now.

It's cool and sweet-smelling in the foyer of the church. The carpet hushes our footsteps and everyone speaks in murmurs. Several men are handing out prayer books and their smiles never falter. Their teeth are exaggeratedly large and white. They outshine the shiny eyes and foreheads.

Mrs. Eagles insists that we go to the front. I feel self-conscious as I trail along behind them. I'm sure it isn't necessary for her to tap her walking stick against each pew as we pass. Everyone is staring at us. Before we sit down, she turns and peers at the rest of the congregation as though she's counting heads. I hunch my shoulders, hoping that people won't see me.

We start off with a hymn. It's something about the petals of the lily being as pure and white as the Lord who made them. I think that that's why I don't like lilies. They're all tied up with death and cemeteries and God.

Mrs. Eagles sings an awfully long amen which carries on after everyone else is finished. I look around quickly to see if other people can hear. My mother nudges me to pay attention.

Someone stands up to read a Lesson. I say to my mother, "Who's that?"

"Dr. Osborne," she whispers back.

Mrs. Eagles says, "Sh-sh-sh" loudly. We're both instantly quiet.

And everyone that heareth my words,
and doth them not, shall be like a
foolish man that built his house
upon the sands.

I think how stupid that is. No one in their right mind would build a house on sand. And then I think of those holiday houses built in the sandhills at Tukutuku. They got washed away in a storm. God must think them foolish men. I want to discuss this with my mother, but Dr. Osborne says, "Let us pray," and everyone bows their head.

While everyone else is praying, I think about the Lesson. It's similar to the story of *The Three Little Pigs*—building houses, having them puffed down because they were made with silly materials. I whisper this to my mother. It wasn't meant to be a loud whisper but several heads from the front row jerk. My mother digs me with her elbow, and on my other side Mrs. Eagles wobbles like the forewarning of an earthquake. Glancing at her, I see her cheeks bulging, pink with laughter. I hunch my shoulders and we giggle together. Then she says, "Sh-sh-sh!" Loudly. Just when the Doctor pauses for effect. I huddle into silence.

They're long prayers full of *thees* and *thous*. Mrs. Eagles drawls out amen after we've finished and keeps her head bowed when we have all raised ours. It's as though she's showing off. I hope I don't have to come with her again.

The service drags on. I've studied the altar, the minister, the carving on the pulpit. The man beyond mother has hairy hands. The lady in front has white scars on the back of her neck. I wonder how they got there—perhaps someone tried to garrotte her the wrong way round so that the knot on the rope was at the back of her neck instead of her throat. That's probably why she comes to church. To thank God for saving her. My eyes become fixed on the stained glass window above the altar.

Ambassadors of Christ, the words say. *Dedicated to our missionaries who during the past centuries carried far and wide the hammer of Christ.*

The people in the side windows look like Arabs and Africans. There are Maoris in the center, judging from their noses and lips. They don't wear Maori clothes but there's a cabbage tree in the background, so they must be. The missionaries are easy to pick out. They're dressed in black, and hold books.

At last it's over. We shuffle out. Mrs. Eagles and my mother talk to Dr. Osborne. I stand and blink in the sunshine.

". . . and this is her daughter, Harper," I hear Mrs. Eagles say.

Dr. Osborne offers his hand and I take it.

It feels like dry bread.

"We haven't seen you at Bible class, Harper," he says.

My insides curl and shrivel as they stand like three sphinxes, beaming at me. I'd prefer to scrub the kitchen floor every Sunday than go to Bible class.

"They are new to the district," Mrs. Eagles says.

"I see. It's on Sunday morning, Harper. At ten o'clock," he says. "We'd be so happy to see you there. Would you like to join us?"

"Oh yes," I lie with enthusiasm.

My mother gives me one of her raised-eyebrow grins from behind her back.

Later, in the car, Mrs. Eagles says, "There is no need for Harper to go to Bible class. It appears that she would prefer not to. Church is really an indulgence for old ladies now. Young ones do not seem to be interested."

I'm amazed to hear my mother laugh.

"It wouldn't do her any harm," she says, "but I don't think she's all that enthusiastic."

"No," says Mrs. Eagles. "Neither do I."

They glance at each other, smiling. There's understanding between them. I sit back and relax, feeling smug. I like people to get on.

We drive through shimmering suburbs. Trees cast blue-black shadows across the sidewalks and heat waves curl up from the bitumen road. Gradually, we climb into the hills above the

79

city to the suburb of Pullmanton where Mrs. Eagles is to have Sunday dinner with her son and his family. It's cooler here. The lawns are green and well-watered. Not like their counterparts in the inner city which are clay-colored and dry. Rich with color, the gardens spill their profusion onto the sidewalks and driveways. It's pretty. It's the elite part of Roxton.

The Eagles live in a large white, Spanish-style house. The driveway sweeps upward between rows of cyprus trees. As we go by, I get flashes of terraced lawns with little brick walls.

My mother swerves and stops at the front door.

"Toot the horn," says Mrs. Eagles.

My mother does so and then, getting out, runs around to open the door for her. As she eases herself out, Mrs. Eagles turns to me and says, "Goodbye, Harper. Thank you for coming to church with an old lady."

"Oh," I say squirming, embarrassed by the unkind thoughts I'd had earlier and the reluctance to accompany her. "That's okay."

The front door opens and a man with a slight paunch comes down the steps. It's Mr. Eagles. He's spruce with Sunday idleness. He looks prosperous. Like his house.

"Hello, Mother. How are you?"

Ignores my mother. Steps right in front of her and takes Mrs. Eagles by the arm, pecking her cheek. Rich people are sometimes rude. My mother doesn't seem to care. She stands passively by.

"Get my walking stick, please, Andy," Mrs. Eagles says in a bossy voice disregarding his greeting.

He frowns slightly and I want to giggle.

"On the front seat," Mrs. Eagles directs him.

He bends into the car, looks at me, says nothing, takes the stick and retreats.

"Thank you, Mrs. O'Leary," I hear Mrs. Eagles saying. "I will be ready for you at four-thirty."

As we drive away, I say, "He's a bit rude. Who does he think he is?"

"Don't worry about him," says my mother. "We've got a whole afternoon to ourselves. What're we going to do with it?"

"You said you'd show me over the big house," I say.

I change into shorts and a top and gallop off to the takeaway for hamburgers and milkshakes. Neither of us feels like cooking. I'm sticky with heat by the time I get back. My mother has spread a rug with cushions under the apple tree. Comfy it looks and I fling myself onto it. We munch and sip, swapping snippets of gossip. . . .

"Did you ever notice that Mrs. Eagles has one nostril bigger than the other?"

"No. But I once knew a boy with one huge earlobe and one tiny weeny one."

"That's okay. There's a boy in my class with one blue eye and one brown one. All the kids call him Two Eyes."

I bite into my hamburger and tomato sauce dribbles onto my leg.

"That's not very kind," says my mother.

"He doesn't care."

She looks at her watch.

"Heavens," she says. "It's quarter past two and I told Mrs. Turbett I'd take the wool over for your jersey. I'd better run."

She dashes off inside. When she comes back she's carrying a parcel. "Tidy up, dear, will you? Do the dishes and make the beds. Give the floor a sweep, too. I won't be long."

I wander inside. She's left an awful lot to do and it's too hot to do any of it. I peer at myself in the mirror. My face is depressing.

It's colorless, when the fashion is for rosy cheeks. Pinch mine and they do brighten up a bit but not in an attractive way. Looks as though I've been crying. Wish she'd let me buy some rouge. Chin's too small and my nose too long. One good thing, I've got huge eyes. But they've got those ugly yellow flecks in them. At least they're not brown eyes. The kid's call me Moo Cow, or something equally unflattering. That's what they call Sonia Smithers, and she's got brown eyes.

There's a pimple on my chin and I squeeze it until it's pink with a tire of white around it. It looks inflamed. I scratch at the center with my fingernail until the blood oozes out. Then I spit onto my handkerchief and dab at it.

"You've definitely ruined your beautiful face now," I say to my reflection.

It pokes its tongue out.

I hear footsteps around the side of the big house. My mother. I rush to make the beds. Only half of one is made by the time she comes in. She pauses at the door, hands gripping hips.

"Why haven't you got this done?" she says. "What on earth have you done to your face? Honestly, Harper! You'll ruin your skin."

She begins to make the other bed, still going on at me.

"Church didn't put you in a very good mood," I say.

"If I hadn't been to church, I'd be beating you over the head," she says.

We laugh.

When the work is finished, we go over to Mrs. Eagles's house. My mother tells me to be careful and not to touch anything. The interior is huge, opulent, and made splendid by the many rich drapes, the ornaments, the glowing warmth of the carved wooden furniture and the beautiful paintings.

I gape, speechless, as we wander from room to room. I'm

intrigued by the high plaster ceilings with domes surrounded by cherubs, bunches of grapes and sheaves of wheat.

"It's like a museum," I whisper and, in spite of the quietness of my voice, it seems to echo through the dimly-lit rooms. I shudder deliciously. "Fancy living here all by yourself. It's so scary I'd get the creeps."

"She uses very little of the house now," says my mother.

"I bet there're ghosts lurking about somewhere."

"Watch out, then," she says. "They might jump out and grab you."

I laugh derisively but inch a little closer to her.

In the dining room I stop before a magnificent ivory figure. It's almost three feet tall and the intricate carving fascinates me.

"That's extremely valuable," says my mother. "It's very old and comes from Istanbul. That's the only one like it in the whole world."

"Whew-ew!" I whistle. "Where's Istan . . . Istabul or whatever it's called?"

"Turkey."

"It reminds me a bit of the one Eric had. Remember?"

"Don't touch it," is all she says.

We don't go upstairs. My mother hasn't even been up there. She says it's been closed since Mrs. Eagles fell down the stairs and broke her hip.

I lean on the bannister, imagining dust and cobwebs with big fat spiders in them. Mice. Bats. Wooden trunks containing porcelain dolls and old fashioned books—musty pages with those squiggly ink illustrations. I suppose there would be brocade dresses rotting in wardrobes, browning handmade lace collars, huge blue ostrich feathers, and brooches of butterfly wings.

We go through the various bedrooms and finally into Mrs.

Eagles's. I've never seen anything like it in my life. It's an enormous room with a bay window. There's space enough for a writing desk and a *chaise longue*. The wardrobe is massive and the bed so high off the ground that I imagine she'd need a ladder to climb into it. But it looks soft, as though packed with birds' feathers under the apricot quilted spread.

My mother opens the side drawers of the walnut dressing table and my eyes leap. There, lying on the moss-green velvet, is an array of jewels that I never imagined possible. I stare, feeling that I'm dreaming, as she drapes them over her fingers, feeding me the names as she takes each one out. One or two she holds up so that they sparkle in the light.

"She must be fan-tast-ically rich," is all I can think of to say.

"She is."

My mother places them all back in the drawers, gently, as though they are babies. She puts the little keys back into the crystal bowl on the dressing table.

"That's the tour completed," she says. "What do you think of all this?"

"Heavens. . . ." I shrug. I can't find words.

"Come on."

She puts an arm over my shoulder and leads me out of the room.

"Your curiosity has been satisfied at last," she says as we wander down the hall toward the kitchen. "Now, remember, Harper, you're not to come in here again."

"I know that," I say. "But what if I'm invited?"

"We'll wait until that happens," she says.

84

·9·

I've only seen Mrs. Eagles to speak to once since we went to church over three months ago, and now I'm to have afternoon tea with hèr. It's my birthday. I said to my mother that I didn't think it would be much fun but she said that I had to go, that I'd enjoy it once I got there and, anyway, it would be rude to refuse after Mrs. Eagles had asked me specially.

I've had a shower and got my hair wet. The ends hang like the straggly pieces of a bird's nest instead of curling upwards as they're meant to. There's another pimple on my chin, red and inflamed because I've been squeezing it. It seems to dominate my whole face.

My mother has left my red vyella skirt with the paisley design and large frill, on a hanger. As I pull it on, I admire the red and green blossoms, commanded by the movement of my body, cascading to the floor.

My mother comes in.

"Do we really have to go?" I say.

"Of course. You should see the things to eat."

She tugs at her smock, is lost in it for a moment and then emerges to fling it onto the bed.

"Have you been baking all day?" I say, brushing my hair, pulling faces at myself in the mirror.

"Don't do that. You look ugly," she says.

There's the crinkle of cellophane as she opens a new pair of panty hose. She pulls them over her hands carefully before putting them on.

My hair is hopeless. It sticks out and refuses to do what I want it to. I change the parting, puff it with my hands. It won't be controlled.

"I'm not going. Look at me," I say angrily, running my fingers through it, stretching it high above my head.

"Here. You look like an old floor mop," and she takes the brush, strokes my hair downwards and into shape. "That's better."

She stands back.

"You look very nice. What're you going to wear around your neck?"

"My new chain," I say.

She gave it to me this morning in a little box wrapped in floral birthday paper. There was a white chrysanthemum cellophaned to the lid and it looked so pretty that it took me ages to decide to open it. Inside, lying among tissue paper, was a gold chain and medallion, not much bigger than a ten cent piece with a bull, Taurus, inscribed on it.

She dropped her maroon jersey dress over her head. I don't like it. It's too severe and old fashioned but it's her best. She turns her back and I pull up the zip.

"Now my turn," I say.

She hangs the chain around my neck and fastens it. We admire each other, saying how super we both look.

Over at the big house, we don't knock but go straight through to the drawing room. As we move down the hall, I begin to feel nervous.

Mrs. Eagles is sitting in her winged chair. Her apricot hair is neat and she's wearing a good dress of pale chiffon and bright orange and cerise flowers on it. The sleeves are enormous and fluttery.

86

"Come over here, Harper," she says. "Right up close so that I can look at you. I will not stand. My leg is bad today."

I say that I'm sorry about her sore leg as I move toward her. There are so many years between us that I feel shy.

"You do look pretty," she says as I stand there feeling gawky. "Have you had a nice day?"

I say, "Yes, thank you," though until this moment it really hasn't been much different to any other day.

"Good. Now pull that stool over near me."

She thumps the arm of her chair to indicate where I'm to sit. Any pretense at being grown up, something my long skirt always makes me feel, flies out the window as I crouch on the stool at her elbow. My mother goes out and I'm left alone with her.

"Did you receive some nice little gifts?" she says.

She's treating me as though I'm a young child, which makes me feel embarrassed. I want to tell her that I'm not a baby.

"Yes, thank you."

"Tell me about them," she says pleasantly, but in that high sing-song voice that adults use for young children.

"There's this," I say, holding the medallion in the palm of my hand. "It's got a sign of the Zodiac on it. See?"

I move closer and she bends forward so that our heads are almost touching. She smells of Vick's vapor rub.

"It's Taurus the bull. That's my sign," I say.

"I hope you do not crash around like a bull," she says, straightening up.

Thinking it's meant to be a joke, I laugh falsely for a long time, hoping to please her. She watches me benevolently and smiles, her pale myopic eyes going watery. It makes her look frail.

"Linda, that's my best friend, gave me a pair. . . ."

I blush. I'm not sure that it would be right to tell Mrs. Eagles

that Linda gave me a pair of bikini pants with three embroidered rabbits on the front.

"What did your little friend give you?" she prompts.

"Oh. Just a pair of . . . a . . . pair of pants," I mutter.

"Very nice," she says. "Of course, we never gave personal
garments as gifts in my day but I believe it is quite acceptable
now."

She's not shocked so I go on.

"Barry, that's my boyfriend. . . ."

"Gracious," she says. "Do you have a young man at your
age?"

"Oh no. He's just a sort of friend," I assure her hurriedly.

The term young man somehow doesn't fit my concept of
Barry. I feel quite justified in denying this assertion.

"I see. Now what did he give you?"

"A fabulous ring," I say. "It's neat."

"Let me see it," she says in an imperious tone.

"I didn't wear it," I say with relief.

It's a band with a silver heart glued onto it. The heart is
engraved with two naked figures, cupid's arrow piercing them.
My mother thinks it's awful and wouldn't let me wear it. I'm
glad about that now. Mrs. Eagles wouldn't approve.

"Do you like jewelry?" she says.

"Yes, it's neat."

We fade into silence. I try to think of something light-
hearted but old-fashioned to say. Mrs. Eagles seems to have
forgotten about me. From the sound of her breathing she could
be alseep but I can't see her face because of the wing of her chair.
Outside, the grey flannel sky makes a backdrop for the bare
branches of the maple tree. The occasional red leaf is glued onto
them and, as I screw up my eyes, I imagine wallpaper. The
silence in the room reminds me of the silence in the detention

room at school. I'm wondering whether this would be a suitable thing to say when she speaks.

"Go to the left-hand drawer in the sideboard and bring me a little red box," she says.

I'm always made nervous by directions such as this, and stupidly begin to open the right-hand, glass-panelled door.

"I did not say door. I said drawer," she calls querulously.

Hot and confused, I immediately begin to open the right-hand drawer.

"Not that one. The other one," she snaps.

She's feeling impatient with me.

"Golly, I'm silly," I laugh, wishing I could vanish.

There doesn't seem to be a red box in the drawer. I rifle through the conglomeration of papers, old napkin rings, tarnished teaspoons, and boxes of every color except red, sticky with embarrassment at my inability to produce the required box. She must think me a nut case. Finally, I take the risk and hold up a purple box.

"That is it," she says. "Close the drawer and bring it here."

She has trouble shaking off the lid. Her fingers are knotty. For a few moments she grapples with whatever's in there and then she produces a brooch. It's oval shaped and old for the silver's tarnished and slightly bent. In the center is an enormous teal-blue stone. She hands it to me.

"Many happy returns," she says. "It is not valuable. I do not think young girls should have precious stones."

The brooch lies in the palm of my hands. I'm surprised and touched by her generosity.

"It is only turquoise," she says. "But it is an old brooch. It belonged to a friend of my mother, a very old lady when I was a girl."

"Thank you very much," I say. "It's really beautiful."

89

And I mean it.

"See that you look after it then," she says. "I wore that brooch when I was about your age. It will remind you of me when I'm gone."

"Gone!"

I look at her and I don't know what to say. I can't imagine her any younger or older or gone. I pin the brooch to my jersey, taking a long time to fill the awkwardness caused by her last remark.

My mother comes in.

"Afternoon tea's ready," she says brightly. "What've you got there? Oh, Harper! You are a lucky girl. It's beautiful."

"It is very small," says Mrs. Eagles, trying to lift herself out of her chair.

My mother stands close at the side of Mrs. Eagles's chair, puts one hand under her armpit and the other under her arm just below her elbow. They heave together and I wait, holding my breath, for the sucking noise as she's extricated, but there is none. With short, slow steps we go through to the dining room.

The table's set with an embroidered linen-cloth. The tea set is of fine pink china, winter sunset with pale birds glazed in flight across it. A canary perches on the nob of the teapot lid, throat stretched toward the ceiling in silent song. Neat crustless sandwiches, dark fruity loaf—a bit crumbly where the butter wouldn't spread, round butterfly cakes in frilled cups, and a large sponge cake splendid in its whipped-cream bonnet, spotted with red maraschino cherries, make my mouth water.

We take our places on the elegant regency chairs, and my mother pours. We go through the motions. We sip and nibble, make polite conversation and smile at proffered plates. They tease me a little about my age and how I'm a young lady. I enjoy the attention, the sophisticated but outdated atmosphere of my party.

Mrs. Eagles asks for a cigarette and my mother passes an Indian lacquered box. She looks odd, smoking. Too old. Halfway through it, she stubs the cigarette out and rises.

"Thank you for a pleasant party," she says, as though she's a guest in our home instead of the other way around. "Goodbye, Harper. Please take that sponge cake home with you. It is much more suited to your figure than to mine."

We laugh and she chuckles at her joke.

She says, "Mrs. O'Leary, no dinner for me tonight, thank you."

She's gone, the big ponderous lady, and as I eat another piece of sponge, relaxed now, holding it with two hands so that I won't drop any of it, I feel real affection for her.

My mother and I clear up. As I carry plates from the dining room to the kitchen, I stuff sandwiches and loaf into my mouth. We're halfway through the dishes when Mr. Turbett, Mrs. Eagles's gardener, knocks on the door. He's supporting a bright yellow bike. I can hardly believe my eyes. How did Mr. Turbett know it was my birthday? He doesn't know us well enough to give me presents. Especially such an expensive one. A bike is something I've wanted for some time. All the kids have them but my mother said they're too expensive. We couldn't afford one. Perhaps he knows how poor we are, I think as I lean in the doorway, mouth stretched into a slice of watermelon.

"This was delivered for you," he says in his slow voice.

My mother looks at him blankly.

I continue to grin.

"Come just now. Delivery van."

"Goodness," says my mother. "Do you know where from?"

"D'know," he shrugs.

"It'll be for me," I say, recovering. "If it wasn't Mr. . . ." I nod in his direction. I don't want to be specific and mention names "You didn't . . . ?"

91

"No," says my mother and then something dawns behind her eyes. She frowns.

"There's an envelope with it," Mr. Turbett says and pulls it from the saddle bag. "The chappy that brought the bike asked me to give you this."

My mother tears it open and pulls out a birthday card.

"Hey! That's for me," I say but she turns away.

"That's mine," I say indignantly.

I lean over her shoulder to take it and before she nudges me away, I read, *With love, Eric.*

"You seem t've sorted that out then," says Mr. Turbett and he ambles off around the side of the house.

"Give it to me. It's mine," I say.

I can't believe that after all this time, Eric has remembered me. How did he know where we live? How did he know that I wanted a bike? It's like a dream.

"May I have it please?" I say, reaching for the card.

She moves away.   .

"It's not for you," she says. "There's been a mistake."

I look at her in astonishment. She's lying to me.

"It's from Eric," I say. "You remember Eric."

"Yes," she says. "I remember Eric."

There's bitterness in her voice. Her face is a mixture of confusion and determination. She draws herself into her leaden, uncompromising posture. Iron glints from her eyes.

"It's going back," is all she says and she marches into the kitchen.

I follow, bewildered.

"You can't do that," I say. "It isn't even yours. It's my bike. Given to me."

"Don't touch that bike," she says.

"I will if I feel like it," I say. "Now, may I have my card, please?"

She's crashing dishes around in the sink. She appears not to have heard me. My hand reaches toward her apron pocket and my birthday card. She slaps it. Hard. I draw back, surprised and hurt.

"I'm sorry," she says but doesn't look at me.

I rub my hand, glaring at her.

"It's got to go back, Harper. We don't accept presents from Eric."

"Why not?"

"Because we don't."

"I'm keeping it."

"It goes back. First thing in the morning."

I open my mouth to protest.

"That's enough," she says. "I don't want to hear another word. The bike goes back to where it came from."

She holds up her hand, daring me. It's hopeless. I know from years of wrangling that when she's made up her mind, the subject is closed. There's no budging her. I'd have more success moving the town hall than getting her to change her mind. I'm overcome with fury.

"To hell with you, you mean, rotten bitch," I scream and rush from the kitchen.

I fling myself onto my bed and howl. I howl because of my mother's stubbornness, her meanness, her inability to confide in me. I howl for Eric and the times when she left me with him in his apartment high above the city. I howl for the bike which was so close to being mine, for the dream that was almost a reality. Me, gliding to school on my brilliant yellow bike, swaggering a little, having the kids swarm around me, perhaps being a little envious. I howl because I don't know who my father is and because I hate my mother and, if I knew who he was, I'd run away and live with him. Because I'm long and skinny, because I have no brothers and sisters. And then I howl for no reason

93

except that it's getting dark. It's that in between night and day time which I hate. It makes me feel lonely.

It's happened before. Once at Thorn's, just before my tenth birthday, I walked in on them in the kitchen. There was an enormous loaf of brown paper on the table from an opened parcel. My mother was holding a brand new leather shoulder bag. She looked upset.

"It'll have to go back," she said. "It's about time this whole business stopped."

They didn't see me in the doorway.

"What is it?" I said.

They turned, startled, naughty children caught in the cookie jar. Thorn snatched a white envelope from the table and tucked it into the pocket of his shirt.

"Well? What is it?"

I moved into the room.

"Nothing," said my mother and quickly rolled the bag up in the paper.

"Who's it for?" I said, thinking I'd discovered what they were giving me for my birthday.

"My sister," said Thorn looking foolish.

My mother glanced gratefully at him.

I knew he was lying.

"Have you got some homework?" she said, wanting to get rid of me.

"Yes. I didn't know Thorn had a sister."

"In Canada," said Thorn.

I looked from one to the other.

"It's for me," I said laughing. "I've caught you. It's for my birthday, isn't it?"

"It isn't," said my mother, "but if you'd like one, I'll get you one."

That puzzled me. I wasn't sure whether they were trying to

94

prevent me from knowing what my present was going to be, or whether there was some other reason for their strange behavior. I caught sight of some wiring on the paper before my mother whipped the bag away to her bedroom and was sure that it had my name on it. I tried to dismiss the niggler that they were deceiving me, but for a long time, it kept rearing up in my mind.

Now I know the truth. The blue bag was for me from Eric. I wonder how many birthday presents have been returned to him. He really must care about me. The thought makes me cry again.

It's dark ?nd my mother hasn't come over from the big house. She has pulled the blind down in the kitchen but I can see her shadow, flat and large, moving across it every now and then. Feeling bad, I suspect, but still unrelenting. She won't give in.

I put on my pajamas and climb into bed. I'll pretend to be alseep when she does come over. Too angry I am. Tight inside. I curl into a ball and lick the snail tracks running down my cheeks.

·10·

"Hey! Look at them," Linda says, grabbing my arm. "D'ya know what they are? They're gay. Camp. They do sort of dirty things."

She giggles, embarrassed, unsure of my reaction but delighted at her superior knowledge.

We're standing in the foyer of the St. James picture theater. We're going to see a five o'clock show of *Lies My Father Told Me*. It's part of my birthday treat. Compensation for the bike, though my mother never said so. She's been nice to me ever since. Letting me do, as far as possible, everything I want. Every now and then she's jabbed with guilt, I imagine, but the surface is smooth. Polished over and we never speak of it. The bike just vanished the day after my birthday. Gone when I arrived home from school.

For a moment, I don't see where Linda's pointing.

"There," she says, pinching my arm. "Those guys. At least, that's what they're supposed to be."

She smirks, hunching her shoulders, fist clenched at her mouth.

"D'you know about them?" she says.

My eyes rove over the groups of people in search of the spectacle that's amusing her so much.

"My father says they should have their things cut off," she whispers. "Some of them pretend to be women. I wonder which one of those two is the woman? I bet it's the skinny one."

I feel my skin flush from the top of my head way down to inside my shoes. It's Eric. He stands out in the crowd so that I wonder how I ever missed him. His blond hair waves down to his shoulders as he throws his head back in that beautiful bird-like curve and laughs. There's a young man with him, pale, tight-looking with thin blue hands and a shoulder bag. Eric is being expansive. He's happy, judging from his gestures, and the young man is clinging to him. Not physically, but in an emotional way. I stare, half-wanting him to see me but terrified that he will.

"They're gay," Linda hisses so that her breath tickles my neck. "You know about them, don't you? They act like men and women. . . ."

"Shut up," I say, wriggling my shoulders irritably to rid myself of her infuriating whisper.

"What's got into you?" she says huffily.

"Nothing. I just don't find that sort of thing funny. That's all."

"Hoo hoo!" she sneers. "I bet you don't even know what I'm talking about."

Eric's looking down at the other man. I can't see his face but there's a caressing quality to his manner and I hate his skinny friend. I want to tear his limp body to shreds and fling it far away. I wish that I were back in the penthouse and it was me he was with. He looks up and his eyes flicker across the crowd. I duck. My scalp burns.

"Look!" shrieks Linda. "He's got his arm around him."

Her fingers nibble at my coat excitedly.

I don't want him to see me. I don't want him to see me with this stupid, simpering girl. If I were on my own, I tell myself, I'd march straight up to him and say, 'Hello, Eric.' But not with Linda. She wouldn't understand. She'd giggle and be embarrassed. Anyway, she doesn't approve of homosexuals.

"Come on. Let's go in," I say.

"Hang on a minute," she says, afraid she might miss something.

She tugs at the back of my coat but I pull free and stride to the ticket box.

"Hey, Harper, hang on," she calls loudly after me.

My neck instinctively pulls into my shoulders. He could have heard my name. He'll know it's me. No one else in the world has the name that I have.

I stand in the queue, face and body swivelled away from the entrance as though I'm spastic. I'm mortified at the thought they might come in and recognize me. What on earth would I say? The row of people moves so slowly, shuffling inch-by-inch toward the box, that I'm almost in tears with impatience. Just before it's my turn to buy tickets. Linda appears at my side and I think, 'Thank goodness, she'll hide me.'

"What'd you rush off like that for?" she says peevishly. "Here. You buy my ticket, I'll buy something to eat."

She pushes her money onto the counter.

"You should've seen them," she grins.

"Don't be so horrible," I say, head still bent.

"What's wrong with watching a pair of silly old queers?"

"Sh-sh-sh," I hiss. "They might hear you."

"Sometimes you're mighty stuck-up, Harper O'Leary," she snaps. "You think you know everything and you don't."

Her face is tinged with pique. Hard little nuts her eyes as she glares at me.

"Why can't you talk about something else for a change?" I say, angry also.

"Hoo hoo! Harper O'Leary likes queers," she scoffs much too loudly, screwing her face at me before prancing off to the candy store.

I turn quickly and see them, Eric and the man, standing at

the end of the queue. They're wrapped up in conversation and don't appear to have heard. My legs nearly melt away all the same, they're so close. I hate Linda for being so stupid and loud. She's mean.

As I stand at the entrance to the theater, she comes up beside me. I don't look back, though I know he's somewhere behind. My shoulders tingle with the thought that his eyes are resting on them, perhaps searching for recognition. Linda's eating a handful of chocolate peanuts, emptying them into her mouth through a funnel made of her hands. She crunches them noisily, deliberately, and it irritates me, though I won't let on. But I eye the packet sideways, and she pretends not to notice. She doesn't offer me any.

We're shown to our seats. I keep my head ducked all the way up the aisle and, to my horror, find that there are two empty seats next to ours. Why didn't we go to another theater? Crouching, as though with cold, I wait restlessly to be swathed in darkness and obscurity.

Linda nudges me and indicates with her eyes that they've come in. I pretend not to know what she means but I see him striding in liquid movements, the other man skipping, hurrying to keep up. They walk past, further up the theater, and I'm both relieved and disappointed.

Strange, I think, biting my fingernail, that Eric should appear after so long. Last week the bike and today I see him for the first time since we left his place over two years ago. I wonder how he feels about the bike being returned. Perhaps that's why he didn't want to know me. He most likely feels insulted.

Psychedelic color flashes Coca-Cola onto the screen, loud sound exhorting us to buy, and the audience sighs into a murmur of rattling paper.

I should feel the same as Linda and my mother about homosexuals. Disgust. But I don't. I understand all about it.

99

Even seen it. Didn't like it that much but can't get worked up about it. Eric doesn't seem to fit into that sort of life even though I know that that's where he belongs. In my mind I dissociate him from it all.

The lights go down and the film starts. At the intermission, Linda wants to buy ice cream. I say that I don't want to. I'm too scared to move. I know that if I stand up, I'll be as conspicuous as a giant at a dwarf's party. He'd be bound to see me. She says she's sorry about what she said outside and goes to buy the ice cream.

She's older than me, Linda, by nearly half a year. Her body is that of a woman, rounded hips and pert little breasts, but sometimes I feel that I've been living centuries longer than she, even though she wears a bra because she has to, and I, because all the other girls do. Sometimes she's so silly that I can't stand her and then she'll do something kind which makes me feel boorish. When she's skittery, I feel ancient and dull. I'm long and flat chested and serious and I wish I wasn't. Wonder why I couldn't grow up in step with myself like everyone else seems to do.

The film is sad. The grandfather dies and I weep copiously, sniffing into my handkerchief. I can hear Linda bawling beside me and the lady behind sobbing that it's the saddest "picha" she's ever seen. When the lights go up, I'm still crying.

"Are my eyes red?" Linda says, rubbing them vigorously.

I keep my head down, howling. She stares at me not knowing what to do.

"It's only a silly old film," she says putting an arm around me. "It's not really true."

"I know," I say and cry some more.

"Heavens," she says, watching the uncontrolled flood in amazement. "Everyone's almost gone. Come on or we'll be thrown out."

"I can't stop," I say and I can't tell her why I'm crying. I hardly know myself.

And then he's there, leaning over the seat in front of me. His hands pull gently at my head. He's trying to raise it.

"Harper," he says. "For goodness sake. Young Harper. And you can't even see me for tears. Do you know who I am?"

"Of course," I say, nodding, sniffing, feeling foolish but not being able to do anything about it.

"Come on, Harper. There's no need to be so upset. It's only a story after all. Do you know what I think when I feel upset by a film?"

I shake my head.

"I think: Bet all those actors and actresses are at home in bed snoring their heads off."

He laughs and the sound is as familiar as my hands and feet.

"I'm silly, aren't I?" I say, wiping my face with my sodden handkerchief.

He shakes out a large crisp one and hands it to me. As I bury my face in it I smell, faintly, his perfume, jasmine. I blow loudly and then don't know what to do with it.

"Keep it," Eric says. "As a memento."

Linda's leaning back against the far arm of her seat. She has recoiled, watching us in horror. I look at Eric, feeling the adoration pouring out of my eyes. I know that I should introduce Linda but she's shocked enough. Anyway, I don't want to share him. For this moment he's mine.

"A hanky for a bike," he says and chuckles.

"You mean you're not hurt or anything?"

"Of course not," he says. "I keep trying and your mother keeps sending them back."

"But how do you know where we live?"

"That's easy. Your mother writes to her mother and she writes to my mother."

Simple.

We grin at each other.

His young man is anxious. He's jiggling restlessly, his face

101

pinched with disapproval as though he doesn't like Eric's attention diverted anywhere else. Linda looks as though she's been dosed with castor oil. I hope she isn't sick.

"You all right now?" Eric says.

I nod.

He doesn't ask about my mother, or how we live, or about school.

"Are we still friends, Bluebird?"

My head bobs puppet-like. I'm speechless.

"Good," he says and touches my cheek gently before he walks away.

The carpet under my feet feels like cloud. Cloud fills my head and chest. I don't feel like me. Linda glares, indignation bursting out of every pore.

"I hate you," she grinds out. "You knew them all the time. You could've told me, you mean thing. Why didn't you?"

"I only know one of them," I say.

We're jostled by a group of people. I lose her for a few seconds. By the time we join up again, I feel in command of the situation.

"How?" she demands. "How do you know a disgusting person like that? My father says they should be locked up."

"He lived next door to us ages ago," I lie. "Anyway, I don't care what your father thinks. They're very nice people."

She strides ahead of me, angry, indignant, probably hurt. Her disapproval is unimportant. I'm riding a wave, sweeping in and out of its curves with ease. Eric cares. Linda and her father and their opinions can fly to the back of the moon for all I care.

"You could've told me," she flings over her shoulder.

I shrug indifferently. It's her turn to sulk.

We sit waiting for the bus in silence. I'm thinking that I won't tell my mother about Eric. It'll be my secret to hug to myself forever. I feel the handkerchief in my pocket and wonder where I'll hide it. Don't know what Linda's thinking but her face is as dark as a winter sky.

When the bus comes, she jumps up and is on it before I reach the door. I sit next to her but her face is turned away from me, pressed against the window. I can see her reflection. She's still angry.

"Honestly, I didn't know it was him," I say. "It's ages since I've seen him. I hardly recognized him."

"You did so."

"I didn't. Honest."

"What about the bike, then. You said it was from your father and that your mother doesn't like him so she made you send it back."

"That's what I thought," I say. "I didn't know it was from him! Anyway, I wasn't even allowed to touch the silly old bike."

She keeps her face turned away, and I try to think of something to distract her. Don't really want this topic pursued any further. I might get caught out.

"I'm going through Mrs. Eagles's place soon," I say. "The very next time they're out. Do you want to see her fabulous jewels?"

She shrugs and half turns toward me.

"My father says they're unnatural."

I don't know what else to say. We sit together but not touching, encased in our separate worlds. The bus cruises on, oblivious to the conflict between us. When we near Linda's stop she pulls the bell cord. I can see the shadowy figure of her father waiting for her.

"Don't tell anyone," I say.

She slides past me, brushing my legs but I can feel her withdraw from contact with me. She doesn't want to touch me.

103

"See you," she says, not looking at me.

Two stops further on, I pull the cord. My mother is waiting for me, hugging her coat across her chest.

"Hello, dear," she smiles as I step down. "Had a nice time? Did you enjoy the film?"

"Yes, it was neat," I say.

"Don't look so happy then," she says. "You look as though you've been to a funeral."

"The grandfather died," I say and burst into tears.

· 11 ·

Mr. Turbett's jabbing away in the polyanthus and tulip bed as I come up the driveway. Spring again and his garden has the fragrance of a florist's shop. Sweet smells mingling with the sharper odor of manure.

"Hello, Mr. Turbett," I call, pushing my head forward tortoise-fashion and fluttering a hand.

He looks up but decides, today, to ignore me. A moody man, sometimes he stops to talk, other days he grunts acknowledgement, but most days he behaves as though I don't exist. Don't force him to speak the way I used to. Once, I'd chatter at him until he'd straighten up and arch his back, rubbing and groaning. In response to my conversation he'd make strange, inarticulate sounds and bob his head. Finally, he'd say, "Off you go, Harper. I've got m'work to do."

He comes here three times a week to do the garden ever since he retired from the City Council four years ago. Dour, he is. Sullen with a narrow pinched face, but his garden is beautifully cultivated, with mounds of sifted earth feeding a multitude of brilliant flowers.

As he isn't feeling conversational, I scuff up the drive and around the big house to our cottage. It's been a long day and I feel tired. The teachers were irritable today. It's probably the sudden burst of heat. They don't seem to understand that sometimes we don't feel like working. Nag, nag, nag all day long. Must've forgotten that they went to school once.

105

Inside, I throw down my case and my cardigan and flop into a chair. My mother's not here and neither is the car in the garage. There's a note on the table. She's taken Mrs. Eagles to Pullmanton and won't be back until nine o'clock tonight. I've got to go to the Turbett place. She'll collect me when she comes home. On no account am I to come home on my own. Before I go, the note says, I'm to take in the washing and fold it. And, I'm to remember to lock the door.

I don't like going to the Turbett place.

"Why can't I stay at home?" I'd say to my mother.

"I'd worry," she'd say.

"I'll be all right on my own. Nothing's going to happen to me here."

"All the same, I'd worry."

"But what on earth could happen? Tell me. What do you think could possibly happen?"

"Nothing, probably, but I'm still not leaving you on your own at night."

We go through this every time. I can't wear her down. I perform and sulk and go to the Turbetts.

I slouch around to the front of the house. Mr. Turbett is still scratching around among the polyanthus.

"Mr. Turbett, I'm to go home with you tonight," I say.

"That's right, Harper," he says.

"What time?"

"When I'm ready."

"Will you come and get me?"

"That's right, lass. Same as always."

"Okay. I'll be ready."

I stand a moment but he's returned to his weeding. The conversation is concluded as far as he's concerned, so I go back to the house, pour myself a glass of orange soda, and cut a thick slice of Madeira cake. It's a bit stale, so I crumble it and throw it to the birds. Mr. Turbett won't like to see crumbs on the path, especially as he doesn't like birds. Hope they've cleaned it up by the time he comes around.

I ring Linda, because we're friends again, and suggest we go through the big house. She has to help her mother and can't come.

I'm bored.

It'd be nice to belong to the Pardon family across the road. I bet they never feel bored. There's so much to do over there. They've got a tennis court and a swimming pool. In the basement, there's a rumpus room with a billiard table and a dart board. The trouble is, they're all older than me, except Nicholas, and he's a spoiled brat. He's in my class at school and he thinks he's smart. Can't even spell properly, but he thinks he's better than everyone else just because his father's a magistrate.

Still, it would be nice to have lots of brothers and sisters. "Harper Pardon."

I giggle because it sounds so dreadful. I'd have to call myself something else.

Samantha? Samantha Pardon. Sam Pardon. Yuk! Lucinda? Katarina? No. Jessica. Jessi spelled with an 'i'? Juliana? Juliana Pardon. Juli for short. Yes. I like that.

There's a scratch on the arm of the chair I'm lounging in. It's deep and shaped like a crescent. Funny that I've never seen it before. I run my fingernail along the groove and wonder how it got there. A dog or a vicious long-clawed cat? Some lunatic, perhaps, brandishing a knife? But, probably, only my mother's knitting needle.

Wonder who my father is. Most times I imagine him to be a Russian aristocrat. Count Dmitri Stubrukovski. He's dark and bearded with deep brown, intense eyes and he wears a fur hat and a mink-lined coat. He is fabulously rich, with a castle in the country and a villa on the Black Sea. He eats caviar for breakfast every single morning, and washes it down with vodka. Other times he's an American rancher who breeds Welsh ponies, a French artist who wanders around Mexico in a big sombrero, with a donkey. Or, occasionally, an English heart surgeon. Once, he was a notorious gangster but that didn't last long. That was after we'd sneaked in to see the movie *Chinatown*. My father looked like Jack Nicholson for a whole week.

Sometimes I get scared at the thought of meeting him. He might be ugly and ordinary, and I'd have to introduce him to all my friends. They might make fun of him. Worse still, he might be like Thorn. I'd die of shame if I had to have someone like him for a father.

It's hard when you can imagine anyone you want for your father. Makes the real thing frightening. Perhaps my mother's right in not telling me. Suppose it is better not to know, though I'd like to see him. Just once.

I've finished my orange drink and the sky has clouded over. I go out and take in the washing. It's neatly hung, the different garments together . . . sheets on the outside of the circular line, pillowcases, tea-towels joined and flapping, underpants, bras, nightgowns . . . very neat my mother is. Efficient. I suppose it's because she was a nurse before she had me.

I stretch and bend, taking down, folding, and placing the wash in the big wicker basket.

Funny, the sizes of our underpants. Mrs. Eagles's look like giant balloons. The sort of thing Gulliver would wear, and my little bikinis what the Lilliputians would wear. I press my face into the crotch of Mrs. Eagles's locknit bloomers and sniff. There's a delicate flavor of soap powder and wind. Mr. Turbett comes around the side of the house carrying a sack of weeds. I

108

think he saw me but he goes on past to the compost heap, as though I'm not here. I feel silly, as I quickly bend over the basket. Don't know why I did it.

Must be careful of the Turbetts. They've got something on me. Mrs. Turbett caught me kissing Barry Jones on the way home from school one day. I feel certain she's told Mr. Turbett, which is why he doesn't speak much anymore.

The day she caught us I was riding Barry's bike across the park, no-hands, and I fell off. Barry must've liked the look of me tangled in his bike because, as I pulled myself free, he leapt on me and kissed me squarely on the lips. His mouth was narrow and hard and I thought I was going to suffocate. Perhaps I would have if Mrs. Turbett hadn't come along and slapped him hard on the backside with her shopping basket. He sat up smartly, hissing with anger. But she wasn't looking at him. She was looking at me.

"Harper, you get along home," she said. "Go'n before I tell your mother."

I looked down and saw that my skirt was crumpled around my waist. I felt foolish, with my underpants uncovered and my navel exposed to the world. Stood up quickly and pulled down my skirt.

Barry rode off. Mrs. Turbett stood glaring at me. There was nothing else to do but to pick up my case and begin walking.

"Straight home, now," she called.

When I turned around her square figure was moving toward the shops. Barry circled the park and skidded to a stop beside me.

"Jeez! What an old dragon," he whistled.

"She'll probably tell my mother," I said.

"She'd better not," he said, running his finger across his throat. I laughed.

109

"Prthurp!" he belched, pulling a face and then, sticking his behind out, he made a loud farting noise in her direction.

Doubling up, clutching my sides, I guffawed helplessly. And then I saw that Mrs. Turbett had turned around and was watching us. Even from that distance I could see that the expression on her face was like an angry Maori carving. Trouble for me if she got near my mother.

It was awkward the next few times I had to go to their place. I wanted to thank Mrs. Turbett for not telling my mother and to say that I was sorry for being rude, but she was difficult to talk to. Tight-lipped and distant. The right moment never seemed to present itself and gradually the incident faded. But I've been careful ever since, remembering my manners, to say please and thank you, and to help with the dishes after dinner.

A cold house, the Turbetts's. A small, weatherboard cottage swept clean to the last speck of dust. Even the street side of their hedge is clean of rubbish.

They rarely speak to each other. When Mr. Turbett gets home, he does his own garden. It's neat—divided into squares like a drafting board. He works right up until Mrs. Turbett calls him in to eat and then after dinner he puts on a woolen cardigan and goes out again to walk along the rows of vegetables or to sit, still as a plaster gnome, on the bench under the fruit trees.

Mrs. Turbett's shaped like a triangle, wide-beamed and narrow-headed. Her eyes are close together like monkey's eyes.

I asked my mother about them.

"They're bored with life and each other," she said. "Marriage does that to people sometimes."

"I'm not getting married then," I said.

Mrs. Turbett has a strange way of saying things. The first time I went there I needed to go to the toilet. Nobody had bothered to tell me where it was. I crossed and uncrossed my legs and tried to think of other things. I jiggled. We were at the dinner table.

"Where's the . . . do you mind if I use your . . . ?" I said at last.

She asked me if I wanted to do "jobbies." I didn't know what she meant. I thought she wanted me to clear the table, or go to the shop for her or to do some other piece of work. I felt terribly embarrassed when I realized.

I told Linda as soon as I got to school the next morning. We laughed about it all day until our class teacher got fed up.

"What on earth's the matter with you two?" he said.

"Nothing, sir," I said and collapsed laughing.

"Linda? What's the joke? Share it with all of us."

"We're laughing about jobs, sir," said Linda.

It was too much. We dissolved into delicious, painful shrieks. The rest of the class tittered.

"If you find jobs so amusing," he said, "you can do some after school."

He put us on emptying trash baskets.

"Jobbies after school," we whispered to each other all through the rest of the day, and then we'd clutch our ribs, stuff handkerchiefs in our mouths, and spill tears of laughter over our books.

Mr. Turbett knocked at the door.

"Are you there, Harper?" he calls.

I'm ready. We go down the driveway together but say nothing. Their house is close. At the corner of our street. I don't take my homework. I'll do it when I get home tonight or in the morning. I'd rather watch Mr. Turbett's color television.

While I was waiting for Mr. Turbett, I did up my face with my mother's makeup, pretending that I was a famous veterinary surgeon, rich and glamorous, and belonging to the international jet set. Barry, handsome, rich and frightfully debonair, was in constant pursuit of me. The last of the afternoon passed quickly and I just had time to put the makeup away and to rub some of it off my face before Mr. Turbett knocked.

As we turn in the Turbetts's gateway, he takes the evening paper from the box. By the time we enter the kitchen, he's flicked it open and is reading. They don't greet each other.

"Hello, Harper," Mrs. Turbett says.

She scrutinizes my face.

"What've you got that muck all over yourself for?"

I can't be bothered explaining that it's not muck. I think it rather suits me and am disappointed that she doesn't think so, too.

"You'll ruin your skin," she says. "I don't know. You young people are all the same. Think you're grown up before you're out of diapers."

She turns back to the sink where she's peeling potatoes. I sit at the table and wait the required time before I can ask to turn television on.

"Are you hungry?" she says. "Tea won't be long."

She always calls it tea. My mother said that a meal of meat and vegetables was called dinner, but that on no account was I to correct Mrs. Turbett. I never know whether to thank her for the tea or for the dinner. Usually, I just say thank you.

We don't speak anymore, and I run my finger over the table top, trying to persuade a lone ant to scuttle on the red markings of the dual-colored formica. The red and cream mixture reminds me of mincemeat.

Mrs. Turbett hasn't much to say anymore—ever since she got noncommittal answers to her prying questions about my mother and our background. Closed down, I did—suburban shops on a Sunday afternoon—when she became inquisitive. Eventually, after calling me close and secretive, she gave up.

She puts the potatoes on to boil and empties the peelings into a bucket under the sink. After dinner, Mr. Turbett will take them out to his compost heap.

"Why don't you wash your hands and turn on television?" she says.

There's the ritualistic hand washing first. I'm afraid to wash them properly in case I dirty the basin, and I never use her towels. If I don't have a handkerchief, I use the hem of my dress. In the sitting room, I sit on one of the maroon-covered chairs with the wooden arms, a crocheted antimacassar protecting the back from the grime of my hair. The Flintstones flash around in their rocky world. I bite my fingernails, watching. From somewhere in the house, comes the sound of Mr. Turbett coughing. He's ready to go out into his garden. He always gives that cough as though he's warning her that he's coming.

Our meal is terrible. It seems unfair that my mother should have to pay four dollars for it. The boiled sausages are coated in a pale thick curry sauce and the mashed potatoes have hard lumps in them. They're cold. We eat in silence except for the clatter of knives and forks on plates.

"It's been a lovely day," I say conversationally.

Mrs. Turbett says, "Yes. It has."

"It'll be good when summer comes," I say.

She says, "Yes. It will."

"I love hot weather, don't you?"

She says, "It makes no difference to me."

He says nothing.

"Are you going away for the holidays?" I say.

She says that they never have holidays.

I give up.

Pudding is no more appetizing than the main course. The custard's sickly sweet and runny and the stewed apples raw. I don't attempt to make conversation again. Instead, I fix my eyes on the cheap bric-a-brac on the sideboard and wonder why Mrs.

Turbett has plastic roses in a vase when there are so many real ones outside. Perhaps Mr. Turbett won't let her touch them.

The silence is relieved when Mr. Turbett says that he'll want his creams for Friday.

She says that he never plays bowls on Fridays.

He says that it's a special tournament.

She asks why he didn't tell her sooner.

He asks if it would've made any difference.

She says that she supposes not and that she'll collect them from the cleaners in the morning.

He doesn't say anything.

Mrs. Turbett and I do the dishes. She washes and I dry. It takes ages because she's so slow. The water in the sink reminds me of the stagnant pond water in the park. It's lukewarm and floating with washed-out food scraps. She puts too much cold in and not enough detergent.

We take cups of tea through to the sitting room. She always has a jar of homemade cookies, which come with us. I settle into my chair for a few hours of uninterrupted television.

"Help yourself, Harper," she says, and I do.

It pleases her. She smiles and rattles them at me.

"I'll have another one, too," she says and soon the jar's empty.

"Just imagine living like that all the time," I say of the Turbetts as my mother and I walk home. "It's so quiet. And her meals. Yuk! One thing, though, it makes me appreciate your cooking. Is that why you make me go there?"

"Of course," she laughs.

She threads her arm through mine and I prattle on, striding left right, left right to keep in time with her.

"It's probably her meals that make them both look constipated," I say and giggle. "That's why they never talk to each other. Constipated all the way to their tongues."

"That's not very nice," says my mother but she's laughing, too.

"Still, she makes jolly nice biscuits," I concede. "You never make. . . ."

It is cosy walking along arm-in-arm, wrapped like a blanket in the darkness. Just my mother and I, with the orange splodges from the street lights for company.

·12·

It's ten o'clock and I can't do my French homework. My
mother's angry. She's sitting opposite me pretending to
read, glasses at the tip of her nose, that business-like look, and
her foot is waggling up and down, up and down. Keeps glancing over at me every few minutes.

She is changeable, like autumn weather. Sunshine one minute, thunder clouds the next.

"Only ten more minutes, Harper, then off to bed."

Pretends to read.

"I don't know why you didn't do that when you came home
from school."

Said that about fifty times.

"Why didn't you do it at the Turbetts's?"

"I told you, I forgot to take it with me," I say.

She sighs and goes back to her book. There's a distracting
chug-chug from the fridge on the porch. It's old and has become
noisy lately. I wish she'd get it fixed. Can't think with that
racket going on.

"Why do you always leave things to the last minute?" she
says a few seconds later.

"I don't."

"God! You make me angry, Harper."

I glare at her. I'm angry, too.

"How do you expect me to get this done if you keep nagging
at me?" I say.

"I'm not nagging and there's no need to speak in that tone of voice," she snaps back.

She's quiet for a while. So's the fridge. It's too quiet.

I look at the strange letter combinations on the page of the text book but don't understand them. There's a stick of dynamite in my chest and the fuse is alight. Any minute now there's going to be an explosion.

"Do it in the morning," she says.

"I won't have time," I say through gritted teeth. "You know that perfectly well."

She sighs again, heavily, exaggeratedly, and picks her fingernails.

'In these tables the verb forms are arranged by person (first, second and third) and by number (singular and plural). The pronoun subjects for the third person singular (*il* / *elle*) and the third person plural (*ils* / *elles*) shows gender. *Ils* refers to a masculine plural subject or to a group of both masculine and feminine; *elles* refers to a feminine plural subject. Change the subject and verb of the following sentences to the plural. Follow the example:

EXAMPLE: *Il va bien.*
Ils vont bien.

There she is in the corner of my eye—pick, pick, pick. There's a ticking noise. I haven't the faintest idea what the book means.

"What does gender mean?" I say, glowering at her.

"I don't know," she says. "Look in the dictionary."

She continues picking her nails. There's a boom in my chest. The dynamite has exploded.

"I can't do it," I shout, banging the book closed. "And all you can do is sit there and pick your shitty nails. Miss Lawrence'll be furious if it isn't done."

On her feet then as quick as a stung rabbit.

117

"Don't you dare speak to me like that," she says, voice harsh with rage. "I think you'd better get off to bed. Right now."

"I'm going to phone Eric."

His name is like an arrow in her chest. She looks at me, stunned. I thump across the room and pick up the telephone directory.

"What'd you say that for?" she says.

"Because Eric can do French. That's why."

"But why Eric? What made you think of him?"

"I told you. He can do French."

I thumb through the directory looking for Robson.

"Stop that. Stop that at once," she screams. "Leave that book alone."

"You can't stop me," I blubber. "You can't even help me."

"Don't be so ridiculous," she snaps. "You can't call people at this hour."

She lunges at the phone book but isn't quick enough. I refuse to relinquish my hold and we struggle, eyes locked like the antlers of stags at mating time.

"Let it go," she says, twisting, flushed. "Why on earth Eric? For God's sake, Harper, what made you think of him?"

She's panting. Her voice high-pitched. Screaming. I'm crying and tugging and she looks as though she'll burst into tears, too, at any minute. Something inside me snaps and I let the book go so that she teeters backward.

"Have you seen him?" she says, arms wrapped around the directory, eyes suspicious.

I move away and turn my back to gather up my homework.

"Have you seen him, Harper?" she says again. "Come on. When? I don't want you hiding things from me."

"Hiding things!"

Swinging around, I face her.

118

I shout, "What about you? You're always hiding things from me."

"That's not true. There's almost nothing you don't know. I tell you just about everything."

"All right then," I challenge. "Tell me. Who's my father?"

Surprised. We both are. Me at saying it, she at hearing it.

"Oh God!"

She sinks into a chair.

"Well? who is it? Why are you hiding that from me?"

"Oh my God!"

She stares in horror, still wrapped around the telephone directory.

"The bastard," she mutters. "Did he tell you? He promised me faithfully he wouldn't."

"Tell me what?"

"That he's . . . about your father."

"Who? Who're you talking about?"

"Eric, of course."

I look at her in amazement. What's she saying? She must be off her head. Homosexuals don't have children. Surely she knows that. What's the matter with her?

"You did know, didn't you?" she says, unsure now.

"I don't know what you're talking about," I say. "Homosexuals don't have children . . . do they?"

"Homo. . . . You know about that as well?" She's shocked.

"Of course I know that."

"I've thought about this so often," she says. "How I was going to tell you about your father."

"Do they?" I insist.

I'm scared.

"Yes," she says. "Sometimes they do."

"Well then?"

119

I can't look at her. My fingers twine and untwine like knitting needles working invisible wool.

She nods. "He's your father."

I don't know what to think.

"Are you sure?"

"Of course," she says. "Quite sure. Eric's your father."

I'm numb. Stunned. Can't think. I look at her and think of Eric.

"And now you know," she says, as though that's final, finished with. There's nothing more to be said about it.

"But how did it happen?" I say. "He's not even as old as you."

"No." Voice starched stiff with bitterness. "He's not."

She looks at me for a long time, obviously trying to make a decision.

"I'll tell you," she says, "seeing you know so much already. Your father Eric—was in the twelfth grade at school when I first met him. We traveled on the same bus. He to school, me to the hospital."

Her voice is gravelly, precise. It's as though she wants to hurt me. I'm paralyzed, frightened by the distance she's put between us.

"I suppose he would have been considered good looking," she goes on, watching me to see how I'm taking it. "Tall. Blond. We started going out together. To parties and such like.

Suddenly her hands reach out grasping air. She shrugs, not knowing how to go on. I relax.

"With a schoolboy?" I say, incredulous, disapproving.

"He was eighteen," she says. "Lots of men are married at eighteen."

Grinning, I look at her, quite liking the idea of one of those huge college boys being . . . related to me.

"But what about . . . you know?" I say.

120

"That!" Scathing voice. "He didn't know until later that he was . . . was . . . homo . . . like that!"

"Eric," I say to myself. "Fancy Eric being my father."

Prowling the room, I run my fingers over flat surfaces, trying to digest this incredible, new identity. Several times I glance at her face to make sure she's not tricking me.

"I'm sorry, Harper," she says, misinterpreting my glances. "I did want you to be old enough to understand before I told you."

I turn on her indignantly.

"I am old enough."

"So it would seem," she mutters, stung.

Suddenly afraid, I say, "Did you want me? Was he pleased?"

"Of course I wanted you," she says, smiling at the fact that I'd acknowledged her. That we were moving onto safer ground. "I was thrilled to bits when I knew you were coming."

"What about him?"

Her face crumbles. She looks at the directory, runs her fingers over the pages.

"Was he?" I say urgently. I must know.

"Not particularly. When he finally found out."

I scowl. Furious.

"Didn't he even know?"

"No."

"But why?"

"It was easier not to tell him. That's why. There was no point."

Angry she's getting. Tired of questions. But I feel resentful. Why's she so mean?

"Bet he would've loved me when I was a baby."

"Probably."

"Why didn't you tell him then?"

"I've just told you. There was no point."

"What'd he say when he found out?"

"Oh God," she groans. "I can't remember."

She's driving me mad. Why did she tell me anything if I'm to get only vague tidbits? Doesn't she understand? This's about me.

"Me!" I shout.

Her head jerks. Eyes widen, startled.

"Try!" I scream. "I want to know."

Tears. Down my throat. In my eyes.

"Please?"

"I'm sorry, dear," she says immediately.

She holds her arms out to me and I curl on the floor close to her leg. I can feel the rounded bone of her knee against my cheek. Her hand strokes my hair.

"He wasn't pleased, Harper. In fact, he was horrified. He wanted nothing to do with us."

"But why?"

She explains then, as though reading from a story book. At first she's detached, as though what she's saying has nothing to do with us.

"Of course, you won't remember any of this. You were too young. We were living with your grandmother and things were becoming a bit strained. Your grandmother had a lot of problems and not enough room. She wanted us to leave but we didn't have much money. So, I took you to see Eric. I thought he might help. But . . . well . . . he had a-a boy . . . a friend living with him." She sighs. A sad sigh, as though all the lights in the world have gone out. "He refused to believe that you were his child. But the friend said that you looked just like him. You had the same eyes."

It pleases me to hear that. That I have Eric's eyes.

"Go on," I say.

"He gave me money and we made a pact. I wouldn't bother him again and he promised never to tell you that he was your father."

122

"That was a bit stupid," I say. "I don't mind him being my father."

"I thought it best."

"I remember," I say, "going to see him. I had on a yellow coat and we went on a bus. Didn't we? I think there were high wooden steps and a ginger cat. How old was I?"

"Nearly three."

"Anyway, go on."

"Well, the arrangement was that he would send me money. Just for you, you understand. I didn't want any of his . . . his. . . . But it didn't last long. About six months or so, if I remember correctly. So! I decided, to hell with Eric. I'd manage on my own."

"But we lived with him," I say. "Remember? After we left that farm."

"I know," she says. "How could I forget? But I was desperate. We had to go somewhere and he was on his own then. It seemed reasonable to expect him to show a little responsibility toward you. Not that that lasted long either."

Her last comment was bitter.

"Never mind," I say, patting her knees, suddenly tickled by the idea. "I've got a father at least."

"Of sorts."

She looks angry, lips curled like dried leaves. I ignore her. I'm delighted.

"Can I ring him and tell him?"

"No," she says quickly. "Harper, you must promise me that you'll never deliberately get in touch with Eric. I'm sorry but, you see, he lives a different sort of life to us. Remember when we lived with him? Those strange people he had there? His funny friends . . . and . . . and. . . ."

She's struggling. Ugly. I don't think I like her at the moment.

"He's my father, though."

123

"Leave it," she says.

"But he's my father!"

She doesn't reply.

"I want to tell him."

"I'm your mother," she says wearily, "and I'm bringing you up. You just do what I say until you're old enough to please yourself. And that means when you're earning your own money. Until then, you're to have nothing to do with Eric. Do you understand me?" She stretches. "And now let's go to bed. It's frightfully late."

Mean bitch, I think. I'll do it one day when you're not here.

"Funny isn't it?" I say, pulling on my pajamas. "I'm not really Harper O'Leary at all. I'm Harper Robson."

She turns her back on me.

I jump into bed and pull the blankets around my chin.

"Harper Robson," I say loud enough for her to hear.

The light switch clicks. I hear her getting into bed in the dark. She didn't kiss me. She doesn't even say goodnight.

· 13 ·

They call me a liar, the kids at school. Say I'm a show-off. They won't believe me when I tell them how my grandmother used to pull the hairs around her nipples out with a pair of tweezers. It's true because I used to watch her through the keyhole in the bathroom door. They don't believe that Mrs. Eagles has jewels like the Crown Jewels of England or that we once lived with a real live sex-pervert. They sneer at me when I say that my father is almost a millionaire. He is, but they reckon I'm lying.

My mother says I'm difficult. She doesn't know what's got into me. I don't know either. There's nothing I like doing anymore. Not even school projects or going to swimming club; going to the pictures with Linda or putting on makeup. Can't even be bothered teasing Mr. Turbett by making him talk to me as I come up the drive. We never speak these days.

The teachers say my work's untidy. They make me repeat it. They don't know what's happened to me either, and they keep nagging at me to pull my socks up, or I'll be in serious trouble. Might even keep me back next year, they say.

So what? I say.

Mrs. Turbett clucks at the pimples on my chin and says it's my age. She says I'll soon be a woman and get my *pinny pain*. She says it as though it's some terrible affliction.

The sun's beating down on my back. It's the first time I've been out in it this year, and my mother said to put oil on and not

125

to get burnt, so I didn't put oil on. I want to get burnt. When she comes out, I'd like to be a wizened, charred stump like the leg of lamb she put in the oven and forgot about. It came out pitch black and so hard that it clanked when it hit the bottom of the garbage pail.

Cried a lot after that night. Not because I'm ashamed that Eric's my father but because I'm not allowed to see him. I'd really like people to see me with him and to know he's my father. He's so tall and good-looking, it'd be neat. I suppose he'd buy me all sorts of fabulous things, too, and take me to exciting places. I think my mother's mean.

There's a narrow trail of ants leading from the fence toward the house and back again. It reminds me of a long black hair. They seem so busy that I envy them. I wonder whether the same ones are going backwards and forwards or whether there's an endless supply so that each one is different and makes the journey only once. I screw one eye closed and put the other close to the ground to see whether I can find any individual markings which will distinguish one from the others. They all look exactly alike, except that some are carrying bigger loads than others, and some don't appear to be carrying anything at all. There must be thousands of them. They continually bump into the oncoming line, pause, doff as though to apologize and then side-step. I push a little mound of earth across their track. The leader stops and the others pile up behind. They vacillate for a moment and then the ones going toward the fence take the right hand side and the ones coming toward the house the left hand side. Nothing's going to deter them . . . like my mother, mouth grim, striding through life, dragging me behind her.

I can hear her talking to someone at the side of the big house. I recognize the laugh. It's Diana Pardon. Can just imagine her in short little shorts that will show off her super olive legs and with her shiny hair bobbing out from her head as she moves.

Diana's sixteen and I don't want to see her. She has a steady

126

boyfriend, Tony Caldwell, who has big ears and smiles a lot, but he's got an old Morris Oxford car which he did up himself. He painted it orange and it's called *The Pumpkin*. They go to tennis club and parties together. Sometimes he's allowed to stay overnight at the Pardons's but he's got to share a room with Nicholas, which can't be much fun.

I'll pretend to be asleep if they come around here. Diana'll think I am awful because my skin's blotchy at the beginning of summer.

"Harper."

"Har-ar-per!"

It's my mother. I put my head down onto my arms and close my eyes.

Diana and I used to sit on Mrs. Eagles's front wall together. I was always flattered that she'd bother. I'm so much younger than she is. Used to think that she was marvellous. Wanted to be just like her. She used to tell me about Tony, how far they went and how he wanted to go further. How she sneaked out with him when her parents thought she was at Creative Dance Classes. They were hopping mad when they found out. Diana was only fourteen then. She's been going steady for two years. They're going to share an apartment when she's eighteen because Tony'll be twenty then and will be getting good money. He's a shop assistant in the furniture department of Allenby's. Her father doesn't like him. Says his eyes are too close together and that he'll never be anything but a salesman. Her mother says that Di will meet lots of nice young people more her own type when she goes to university. Diana says she's not going to university. She's going to have a baby instead. I said that I didn't think she should. She should ask her mother about it first. She said not to be so stupid and she climbed down from the wall and went home. I hated Di thinking I was stupid.

"Har-ar-per."

I ignore my mother's call.

127

The last time Di and I sat on the wall together, Mrs. Pardon came to the gate. She yelled to us that we looked like a pair of gossipy old crows, which made us laugh. She didn't say, "Get down from there at once," as Mrs. Turbett would. Mr. Pardon strolled out and joined her. He had on a pair of cream trousers and an orange shirt. He was going to golf. I watched them talking and for some strange reason, I got a lump in my throat. Soon Nicholas came out and said something to his father. Mr. Pardon turned on him grinning and punched the air around his head. Nicholas ducked and hit his father in the ribs. Mr. Pardon fell back and pretended to be hurt. Everyone laughed and poked fun at him. Watching them made me feel so lonely that I wanted to cry. I told Diana that she was lucky to belong to such a super family but she just shrugged and said that Nicholas was a little shit and she'd give him away anytime except that no one would want him. She didn't really understand what I meant.

The talking's stopped so Diana must've gone. I'm glad she didn't come to see me.

The poor cabbage leaves are floppy. Puppies' ears. I'd like to give them some water but Mr. Turbett said that you must never water plants in the middle of the day. I asked him why not but he just said, "Because I say so. Now off you go."

There are footsteps coming around the side of the big house. My mother. I grab my book and pretend to read.

"I've just been talking to Di," she says. "Why didn't you come and say hello?"

Pretend not to hear her.

"Harper!"

Turn the page of my book.

"I know jolly well you're not deaf," she says. "Would you mind answering when I speak to you."

She comes along the path, angry voiced, shadow cutting across my back.

"Harper, I'm fed up with your behavior," she snaps. "Would you look at me when I'm talking to you. And cut out your sulking, my girl. I could slap you, you make me so mad."

She'd do it, too, from the sound of her. Vulnerable with my backside in the air. Flick over quickly. Pull my knees up and wind my arms around them. Everything tucked in and safe.

"Didn't you hear me call?" she says angrily.

"When?"

"Just now. A few minutes ago when Diana was here."

"I would've come if I'd heard you, wouldn't I?"

I draw back a little. Sound ruder than I intended and she moves toward me as though to deliver one of her hefty slaps. But she changes her tack and sitting down beside me, smiles in a friendly way.

"Guess what Di wanted?"

Oh heck! One of her guessing games.

"How would I know? I wasn't there."

"Well, guess."

"Uhm. I can't," I say and think, why can't she just come out with it? Why does she have to make such a mystery out of everything?

"You'll never guess," she laughs, "so I'll tell you. She's having a party on Saturday night and you're invited."

She's watching my face, pleased, I can tell from the glow in her eyes, which anticipate my delight. But it's not delight I feel. It's panic.

"There are about forty people going," she says. "Lot of them you'll know. Like the Ennis girls and Douglas and Fiona Stewart and, of course, Nicholas and. . . ."

"I'm not going," I say.

She stares at me as though I'm some aberration she's never seen before.

"Of course you're going. Don't be so silly. You'll love it."

"I'm not going," I say.

She sighs. That plea-for-patience sort of sigh.

"Honestly, dear, you'll enjoy it. It's a pool-and-games party. You love swimming."

"I told you, I'm not going. The Pardons are snobs and, anyway, I hate Fiona Stewart."

Picking up my book I flick my thumb across the pages. Wish she'd leave me alone.

"That's news to me," she says. "You've always liked the Pardons until now. I think you should make an effort and go. It was nice of Diana to ask you and it'd be rude to refuse."

I know she's right. It's difficult to explain how I feel, how those people make me feel like a freak these days. Anyway, she'd just tell me to get in there and show them that I'm as good as they are, because, she'd say, I am. She might think she is but I know I'm not.

"Anyway, I haven't got anything to wear," I say.

"You've got lots of nice clothes," she says.

We're silent. She plucks blades of grass thoughtfully.

"Tell you what," she says, changing course again. "I'll buy you a new dress. How's that? You go to the party and we'll go into town on Tuesday afternoon and get something really fabulous."

"Nobody wears party dresses. Don't you even know that yet?" I say.

She sighs and mutters "Oh God" but perseveres.

"A sunfrock then?"

Blackmail but tempting. Haven't had anything new for ages. Then I think of all the new things I've been conned with in the past. We never have enough money to buy anything I like. It's always something cheap that needs altering. I have to admit that my mother is clever at disguising the ill-fitting, bargain

130

look about my clothes but the agonies we go through to achieve this!

I visualize myself standing on the table while she, hedgehog mouthed, jabs pins at me. . . .

"For goodness sake, stand up straight!"

"Hold your stomach in Harper."

"Stop slouching or the hem'll be crooked."

Hours of snipping and bad temper because she doesn't like sewing. She only does it to economize. I can't be bothered. It isn't worth it.

"I don't want a new dress," I say, "and I'm not going to Diana's party."

"Think about it for a while," she says, getting up. "You might change your mind."

I don't change my mind, but by Saturday afternoon I feel pretty bad about it. At five o'clock, I wander around to the front of the big house. The party will have started by now. I climb onto the wall and sit in my secret place where the silver birch tree hangs over onto the sidewalk. No one can see me.

I had told Linda about the party and had said that I wouldn't go because she hadn't been invited. I knew it wasn't true but it made me feel better for a while, having her agree that she wouldn't have gone either if they'd invited her instead of me.

My mother's disgusted with me. She's so angry she can hardly speak.

Although the Pardons's house is quite a long way from the street, music blares out. It's Rod Stewart. "Stay away from my back door," he sings and I wriggle on my wall in time to the song.

Two cars drive up. One parks out on the grass verge opposite, the other turns into our driveway, backs out and parks so close to where I'm sitting that I'm afraid I'll be seen. Kids get out, chatting, attention focused on the house across the road. They haven't noticed me. Nicholas is at the gate, scrubbed-looking with his hair swept back and damp. Di comes out.

"Hi," she shouts, waving.

She looks gorgeous in a white wrap-around cotton knit top, bare midriff and a long red and white skirt. I'm glad I didn't go. The kids in the car are older than me, the girls slim and shiny, the boys casual but assured.

Susie Wells is among them. She has extravagant gestures, Susie, always flinging her arms in the air. As she crosses the road, she swings her Greek shoulder bag around her head like a lasso, at Diana. It flies out of her hand, sails through the air and lands against the wall just below where I'm sitting.

"Trust me. I've done it again," she laughs and comes over to retrieve it.

As she straightens up, she looks into the tree. Into my eyes. I've pulled my knees up so that I'm hunched and small. I feel like a cat that's suddenly confronted by a large dog.

"Shit, you gave me a fright," she says. "What're you doing up there? Do you think you're a bird or something?"

I keep staring.

"Come on, Susie" someone yells. "The party's this way."

"Coming," she shouts, laughing and, forgetting me, runs across the road.

I watch, tingling with embarrassment as they fade into the driveway.

It's getting dark. The sky changes into a clear cellophane smoothness. One white star and a small crescent moon sit as though cut-outs pinned onto it.

"Tonight's the night,

Everything's gonna be all right" . . . Rod Stewart assures the world from the tape deck.

132

"Liar," I whisper and then I'm crying because, all the time, I wanted to go. I feel silly sitting here, especially now that Susie has seen me. I imagine her entertaining everyone at the party, with lots of miming and exaggeration, about the nutty kid across the road sitting in the tree like a sparrow. The Pardons will know it's me. They'll think I'm strange and bad-mannered.

"Har-ar-per."

My mother!

Quickly I rub my face with the hem of my dress and slip out of the tree. I don't want her to find my hiding place or to know I've been crying. By the time she comes around to the front, I'm scuffing up the drive.

"There you are," she says. "Dinner's ready."

She'll see my swollen eyes. I watch my feet.

"Piker," she grins, slinging an arm over my shoulder. "Guess what we're having for dinner?"

"I don't know," I shrug.

"Chicken. And then I'll beat you at Scrabble."

"No you won't," I say and we race each other up the drive.

·14·

"What if they come home early?" Linda whispers behind me as I try the kitchen door to the big house. "Scared?"

"It's breaking and entering," she says. "We'll be in real trouble if we're caught."

I turn the handle slowly. The door creaks open.

"It's not even locked," I say. "Hardly call that breaking."

"But what if Mr. Turbett catches us, Harper? He'll tell."

"Don't worry. He's working around the front. Anyway, I reckon he's as deaf as his old spade."

"I don't think we should," Linda hisses.

I turn on her, beginning to feel exasperated. She's seen the turquoise brooch Mrs. Eagles gave me for my birthday. I know she envied it as she admired it. I bragged about Mrs. Eagles's jewels. Couldn't help it. About the diamonds cascading like Belgium lace, the rubies, sapphires as big and as blue as her eyes, emeralds green like new leaves on the apple trees, the cameos, garnets, topaz—amber-like smooth globules of toffee—gold chains, silver filigree as fine as spider webs.

She didn't believe me. "Prove it," she kept saying. "Take me there and show me and then I'll believe you. You're always exaggerating, Harper O'Leary."

Nagged at me every day to show her. And now she's piking—the scaredy cat.

"Do you want to or don't you? Hurry up and decide, because if you don't I've got other things to do," I say, impatiently.

I push the door wider open. The kitchen looms dim, clinical and empty. I tiptoe across the polished linoleum.

"Come on," I say. "Hurry up. And close the door."

She follows at my elbows, eyes popping like a pair of striped candies. The thought makes me giggle. Her fear gives me courage. As we move down the hall, a Venetian blind clatters and she jumps, clutching the sleeve of my cardigan.

"What was that?"

She tries to pull me back.

"I hate this," she says.

"It was your idea."

"I've changed my mind. Let's get out of here."

"Just have a look in the dining room," I say. "Here, come and look at the ivory statue."

Pushing the heavy oak door open, I tiptoe in. I know that the finely carved figure of the Goddess Shiva will mean nothing to her, that she'll probably think it's plastic, but I want to keep her here, to prove that I'm not a liar.

"Isn't it just fabulous?" I say, touching the figure with reverence, but she's not impressed. She's ogling the intricately decorated sherry decanter on the sideboard.

"Wow! Harper, isn't this beautiful. Look at all this gold. Is it real?"

"Of course," I say. "Want a drink?"

I pull the stopper out nonchalantly and fill two goblets while she watches nervously. I've tasted alcohol before and because I know Linda hasn't I feel superior. I know I like sherry. My mother often let me sip from her glass when she poured herself one in the evenings.

Casually I toss mine back. It's thick and sweet. Linda sips hers guiltily, looking at me with scared eyes.

135

"Go on," I say. "I'm going to have another one."

She giggles and empties her glass.

I refill it.

"We'd better not have any more," she says. "They'll notice. Look, it's nearly half-empty."

"I'll put some water in it like the French people do," I say.

She chortles and, upturning her glass, drinks it down.

"It's rather yummy," she says. "I'll have just an eensie bit more."

So we have a third and then a fourth.

The room is teetering slightly. I take the decanter into the kitchen and fill it with water. The color is pale amber not the rich golden syrup color it was before. But we kid ourselves that no one will know the difference.

My head is spinning and my eyes won't focus properly. Linda's talking to the cherubs on the ceiling.

"Hi ya, little fat arse."

I've never heard her speak like that before.

"Hey, Lin," I say, "want to see the jewels?"

"Of course," she says, prancing around the table like an oversized pixie. "When I've finished dancing with big boobs and wobble arse."

I grab her arm and we stagger down the hall, giggling weakly.

"What if your mother comes home?"

Laughter.

"Mrs. Eagles'd die of shock."

We clutch each other, convulsed.

"Old Turbett'd swallow his false teeth."

Pain in my ribs and tears from laughing.

It's delicious.

Mrs. Eagles's bedroom is at the far end. Linda's skittery as I open the door, hopping on one foot and then the other, arms like shivery grass.

"Wow!" she says as her eyes rove the the large opulent room.

I climb onto the bed and bounce up and down. It's huge and soft as though the mattresses are made of cottonwool. I'm sure there must be at least three of them. Linda climbs on and joins me. We toss as though on a trampoline until puffed, then lie there dizzy and exhausted.

"We'd better get off," she says suddenly, a brief moment of guilt breaking through the sherry haze. She moves toward the door as though to rush out. I climb down quickly and open the wardrobe doors. I'm anxious to keep her here.

"Jeez! Look at these."

Curiosity.

She comes and we peer at the large mottled skins of fur hanging there. I touch them, counting—four.

"Feel them," I say. "Gosh! They feel beautiful."

I snuggle my face into the coats but Linda won't. She stands with a strange disbelieving look on her face. There are dresses, too, all soft, bright fabrics hanging limply. And shoes, neatly paired, toes facing the brick wall.

"She must be awfully rich," Linda whispers.

"I told you she was, but wait 'til you see these."

I close the wardrobe doors and take the little keys out of the crystal bowl on the dressing table. Opening one of the drawers, I drape a ruby and a diamond necklace over my fingers.

"Shit," she says softly.

She puts her hand out as though to touch it and then withdraws. She looks as though she believes it will crumble or vanish if she breathes too heavily.

"What about these?"

I draw out a handful of rings and slide them on my fingers.

They're far too large for my hands but the effect is impressive.

"Crikey."

Her eyes look as though they're about to fall out of their sockets.

"You have to have pierced ears for the earrings."

I dangle a cluster in front of her nose. She takes them, fingering them lightly.

I open another drawer and then the two on the other side of the mirror. She's relaxed now, distracted. We drape ourselves in the jewels, parading, giggling helplessly. I go to the wardrobe and pull on a fur coat. It drags on the carpet and is heavy.

I'm in my element. All my life I've loved dressing up. When I was a little kid, I'd amuse myself for hours draping my mother's clothes over me, scraping down the street in large high-heeled shoes, handbag slapping my knees, lipstick smudged on my face. People I met invariably played along with me.

"I'm Mrs. Brown," I'd say.

"How do you do. You do look smart," some strange lady would smile.

"I'm going to the shops today," I'd tell her.

Linda and I first became friendly because she has a large box of old evening dresses and shawls and shoes. She has the equipment and I the ideas on how to use it.

"Bow to the Queen of Persia," I say now in a false voice, arm to the back of my neck, sauntering around the room.

Linda explodes laughing. She goes to the wardrobe and drags one of Mrs. Eagles's dresses over her head.

"Bow to me or I'll have your head chopped off. I'm Elizabeth the First of England."

Grabbing the silver-backed brush from the dressing table, she pretends to chop off my head. We gurgle helplessly.

138

"I'm Olivia Newton-John," I say. "Show me some respect or I'll send John Travolta to sort you out."

"Oooh! Yummy. I'd better get my best gear on for that," and flinging the dress over her head, she pulls her skirt off her shoulders and starts decking herself with more jewels.

Laugh! Hiccoughy laughter with tears and sore ribs.

"Imagine what Miss Lawrence would say."

"Bonjour, madame. . . ."

"Would you like a ruby. . . ?"

"As a memento?"

"As a bribe. . . ?"

"To choke yourself on. . . . Oh help! Oh Christ!"

Suddenly she's ripping the jewels from her hair, from around her neck, frantic, panicky actions, flinging them down any old how on the dressing table . . . I bellow with laughter. She starts to scream.

"Hey, don't make so much . . ." I say, and then I see Mrs. Eagles standing in the doorway. She's leaning on her walking stick and has two bright, red patches on her cheeks. She opens and closes her mouth, trying to speak, reminding me of one of those ungainly tropical fish we saw at the aquarium. And then I'm rigid with fear. Linda rushes from the room, knocking against Mrs. Eagles in her dash for safety. Her screams record her progress out of the house and down the driveway.

Suddenly I'm talking, insanely, jabbering with no idea what I'm saying. I'm tearing jewels off my body, poking them back into the drawers, one eye on Mrs. Eagles's reflection in the mirror. I'm terrified of the big figure blocking the only means of escape. I wish she'd say something. Hit me even, but not just stand there with her eyes bulging and those clownish pink spots on her cheeks.

There's only one other occasion that I can remember being

139

gripped by such fear. But even that was different because I was propelled into a flurry of action caused by rage. It was the night that my mother, after weeks of nagging at him, called Thorn a "mean cringing bastard." He moved swiftly around the table and with the back of his hand, whacked her across the face. Then he did it again. To the other cheek. This time with such force that she fell off her chair. I was paralyzed with shock and fear. Then I threw myself at him, punching and kicking, screaming for him to leave my mother alone, furious that he should dare to touch her in such a way.

But this situation is not the same. My fear is partly from being caught, but mostly from the shock and the uncertainty of Mrs. Eagles's intentions.

"You're home. You knew we were here all the time!" I shout hysterically.

I'm accusing her. As though it's her fault that I'm trapped. Her heads nod woodenly, affirming my reproof.

Her voice, when she speaks, is soft. Hardly audible.

"Harper . . . please. . . ."

Her eyes move toward the bed.

"Help me . . . please . . . doctor. . . ."

There's panic in her eyes and a new panic for me, too. A cold fear for the lady standing. I move towards her but am not quick enough. Slowly, heavily, like a dollop of treacle sliding from a spoon, she slithers down the wall and falls onto the carpet.

I'm transfixed, horrified, rooted to the spot in astonishment. I hear scream after scream but don't know where the noise is coming from. The body doesn't move and I can't get out. I'm afraid to go any closer. I don't know what to do.

Mr. Turbett suddenly appears in the doorway, boots caked in mud, his gardening fork splattering freckles of dirt over the inert body.

"She's dead. She's dead," I scream. "She just fell down dead."
I'm shivering and crying.

"Gawd," he says in his slow voice.

His shrewd eyes screw up and almost disappear as he stares at me. I wonder why he doesn't do something instead of standing there like a great clod of the dirt he's always digging. My panic makes me frantic.

"She's dead. Do something," I scream in rage.

"All right," he says bending over Mrs. Eagles. "No need to go off y'head."

He takes her wrist in his dirty hand and holds it for a few seconds, listening intently. My hands are across my mouth, heart sledge-hammering. I glance out the window impatiently. The sky's blue. Blue! It should be black, draped in funeral clothes, striped with anger and tears. He's taking ages.

"Please God," I pray silently, "let her be all right. Please don't let her die, and make Mr. Turbett hurry up."

Silence. I hold my breath until I'm going to burst.

"Is she all right?" I say, unable to contain myself any longer.

"Not yet," he says, looking suspiciously at me. "Run and get the wife. Quick."

I'm incapable of moving.

"Get," he says ferociously, and raising an arm moves as though he's going to hit me.

His threat is what I need. The urgency of the situation penetrates my confused brain and I scuttle past the large, sad body.

Once outside, I race down the street toward the Turbetts's house, sobbing. My head reels and my stomach is churning. There's a vile acid taste in my mouth and my eyes water. I'm going to be sick, I think, and then I am. I spew hot half-digested, sherry-soaked vomit. My nose and eyes stream and I feel that everything inside me from my toes upward will end up in the gutter. I haven't got a handkerchief. Wiping my mouth and nose on my shirt and my hands on the back of my jeans, I run on. My forehead feels as though I'm banging it against the sharp edge of a window sash.

"Mrs. Turbett," I shout and rush in without knocking.

She's in the sitting room, knitting, watching the afternoon's soap opera on television.

"You've got to come quickly," I gasp. "Mrs. Eagles nearly. . . ." I fight the lump in my throat, the tears in my eyes. "Dead."

"What are you saying, Harper?" she says, putting her knitting down.

Then she wrinkles her nose in disgust and stares at my vomit-stained clothes.

"You've been sick," she says. "What are you doing running around the streets in that state? Have you been drinking?"

"No. Yes, please come quickly. Mrs. Eagles's very ill."

"Why didn't you clean yourself up?" she demands. "You'd better come through to the bathroom. . . ."

"Mrs. Eagles's dying," I shout. "My mother isn't home."

The stupidity of the woman nearly drives me mad. She stares at me as though the words refuse to penetrate.

"Mr. Turbett wants you. He said you're to come at once."

"Gracious," she says. "I won't be a second."

She rolls her wool and tucks it into her knitting bag. I turn off the television. She takes a comb from the mantlepiece and pulls it through her hair. She changes her slippers for a pair of walking shoes, locks the back door and hides the key under a brick near the trash bag. She's so slow I want to pummel her.

When we arrive at the big house, I see that the car is in the garage. My mother's back. We find her and Mr. Turbett in the hall outside Mrs. Eagles's bedroom. They stop talking when we enter. My mother looks at me reproachfully. Mr. Turbett looks angry and accusing.

"How is she?" Mrs. Turbett says in a flutter of anxiety.

"She's comfortable," says my mother. "She's had a nasty turn and she's not well, poor old lady."

"What a shame," clucks Mrs. Turbett, and I imagine that she's already donning funeral black.

"It's her fault," says Mr. Turbett glaring at me. "Her and her friend were in the old lady's bedroom. Goodness knows what they were up to, and the old lady goes in and catches them, and she got such a shock that she fell down with a heart attack."

I look from one to the other.

"That's not true," I say.

"You was in there," he says.

"Yes, but. . . ."

My mother rests her hand on his arm to silence him.

"The doctor'll be here any minute," she says. "We don't want him to find us outside Mrs. Eagles's door arguing."

"Still . . ." he says, reluctant to give up.

My mother looks at Mrs. Turbett.

"How about making us all a cup of tea?" she says. "I think we need one."

"That's a good idea," Mrs. Turbett says, pleased to be useful and she thuds down the hall toward the kitchen. Mr. Turbett follows.

We've had crises before, my mother and I. Like the time granny was knocked over in the street and came home in an ambulance. But I wasn't really involved, I just hovered and gawked while the adults ran from the bathroom to the bedroom with anxious faces and I got hungrier and hungrier because nobody remembered to cook that night. And, too, there was the time that the Reverend Wilkins cut the tip of his finger off with the axe. And the awful night Eric fainted, hitting his head on the edge of the bench. There was so much blood, I thought he'd bled to death. But this's different. This's the first time something of such enormity has happened because of me.

"Will she be all right?" I say to my mother.

"I don't know," she says and she looks worried. "I think she'll pull through but it's hard to say."

The doorbell rings.

The doctor.

As my mother rushes past me to open the door she says, "Harper, go home and have a shower, dear. You smell atrocious. You can tell me what happened when I come over."

"Was it my fault?" I say, rooted to the spot.

"No," she says, "No. Mrs. Eagles didn't go to bridge today because she wasn't feeling well. I guess it would've happened anyway. Now, off you go."

The Turbetts stop me as I go through the kitchen.

"You're a wicked girl," Mrs. Turbett starts straight in. "Look at you. All covered in sick."

"You should've heard the screamin'," he says, "Like they was skinnin' a live pig."

She gives him a withering look. He sucks his tea noisily. I begin to cry.

"You nearly killed that old lady," she says.

"What were you doin' in there? That's what I want to know?" he says.

"Just looking," I blubber.

"If your mother only knew what you get up to," Mrs. Turbett says shaking her head, gripping her hips, beady gaze bouncing off my tears.

"You should've seen the other one scampering down the drive," he chuckles.

She glares at him. I slosh tears into my handkerchief.

144

"It's too late to cry," Mrs. Turbett says, refilling her cup. "Poor old dear."

"It wasn't my fault . . ." I begin.

She looks at me disbelievingly.

"No, Harper," she says. "Don't make it worse by denying it. We all know what went on."

"But that's not right. . . ."

My mother comes in. Her face is creased with worry.

"Mrs. Eagles has had another stroke," she says. "She'll have to go to the hospital. The ambulance is on its way. I'll go with her. . . ."

Mrs. Turbett tich-tiches.

"You'd like Harper to come home with us?" she says.

My mother ignores that.

"I was wondering," she says, "whether you would get in touch with Mrs. Eagles's son for me. Just tell him what's happened and that she's in good hands. She'll be going to St. Luke's. Perhaps he'd better go straight there. I must go and pack her a few things. Would you mind? You know him, don't you?"

"Of course, luv," says Mrs. Turbett. "No trouble at all. I'll phone him right away."

My mother rushes to the door. She pauses.

"Harper. . . ."

"She can come home with us," says Mrs. Turbett.

I look at my mother, pleadingly.

"That's kind of you," she says, "but Harper will be all right on her own for a little while."

I give her a grateful smile as she ducks out.

I cook omelets for tea. My mother said that she didn't want anything to eat but I'm doing it anyway. I want to be kind and to make up for the awful things I've done lately.

It's dark outside and the sky, splattered with stars, looks infinitely sad. I keep imagining long silent corridors, white-clad nurses gliding like ghosts, and in a high, green-painted hospital bed, a large old lady struggling for her life.

My mother's sprawled in an armchair drinking gin. She hasn't even taken her coat off. I've never seen her drink gin on her own before. She's at her wits end, she said. If I carry on the way I'm going, she doesn't know how I'll end up. I'll turn out a criminal, she said.

I had to tell her. About Linda and the sherry and the jewels. Have to spend my next two weeks' pocket money on a bottle of sherry to replace the one we drank. I don't mind that. My mother said that she was ashamed to have a daughter who was such a weak little fool. Haven't I got a mind of my own? she wanted to know. Do I have to do everything my friends tell me? It seems that I do.

After she'd raved on a bit, she simmered down, because I was crying. She said not to worry about the Turbetts. She'd tell them that it wasn't my fault that Mrs. Eagles had the stroke. Mrs. Eagles would have had it anyway, she said, but that didn't excuse me for what I did. . . . I know that.

There are things I need clarified. I ask her.

She says, "Mrs. Eagles needed some new underwear. It'd been ordered for ages and had arrived in the shop today. I went to collect it. That's why I wasn't home. Otherwise none of this would have happened."

Did I make her have the stroke?

"No." My mother sounds weary. "From your account of what you were doing and the noise you must've been making, she would be quite aware of the fact that you were in the house. I guess it didn't improve her condition, though."

Did my mother think that Mrs. Eagles came into the bedroom to catch us? I'm biting my little fingernail.

146

She sighs. "If she'd wanted to catch you, I imagine she'd have gone into the dining room when you were creating that racket. No. I think she wanted you to help her. Perhaps put her to bed or get a hot water bottle or something."

I feel terrible.

I hand her a plate with an omelet and a piece of bread and butter on it. She fiddles with the food, pushing it around, nibbling. Feels bad about Mrs. Eagles, it seems. Blames herself for not being there when it happened.

·15·

It's the summer holidays and nearly two weeks since Mrs. Eagles went into the hospital. We've hardly heard a word about her. Not even from her son though my mother has rung him several times and left messages for him to get in touch with her. He hasn't and we worry.

She rings the hospital often, too, but it's always the same; "Mrs. Eagles's progress is satisfactory." "Mrs. Eagles is comfortable."

We don't know what to do. We're living here without Mrs. Eagles to justify it. It seems strange, as though we're squatters and one day the police will come and chase us away.

My mother goes over to the big house every day to dust and open the windows. She's spring-cleaned the place several times although it doesn't need it. It seems that she must have something to do. She feels lost, as I do.

No one has bothered to pay her.

Two days after Mrs. Eagles was rushed to hospital, we went to visit her. St. Luke's is a posh, private hospital on the other side of town and we had to take a bus into the city and then another out to the highland suburbs where the hospital is. At the city bus stop, there was a woman selling flowers, so my mother bought a bunch of pink carnations. She complained about how expensive they were, which made me feel guilty. I couldn't even

148

offer to pay for some of them because I hadn't had any pocket money for ages. She handed them to me, however, and said that I could give them to Mrs. Eagles.

There was no one at the reception desk when we arrived. In fact, the place seemed deserted. Everything was sunny, polished, with huge vases of flowers and an autumn-patterned carpet. But silent. I felt that I was stepping into the beginning of a TV thriller.

My mother said, "Come on, we'll find her ourselves." Unperturbed by the lack of people, she darted off down the corridor, around a corner and without knocking but muttering that this was the room they'd admitted her to, threw the door open. I was close behind her and was startled to see, instead of Mrs. Eagles, a thin old man in striped pajamas, melting into a stack of pillows.

"I'm sorry," said my mother chirpily. "Wrong room."

The man made no movement. I don't think he was aware of our intrusion.

As we zig-zagged down the corridor reading the name tags outside each door, I wondered whether Mrs. Eagles had changed much. Perhaps I wouldn't recognize her even though my mother had warned me that her right side was paralyzed and she wouldn't be able to talk or move much. I hoped that when she saw me, she wouldn't have another stroke. I visualized her plum-colored eyelids fluttering, eyes bulging, her body rolling across the bed and falling, thud, on the floor.

"Let's go," I said. "When Mr. Eagles gets in touch he'll be able to tell us where she is."

"After coming all this way?" said my mother.

A nurse materialized.

"Can I help you?" she said.

My mother smiled. Confident.

"We're looking for Mrs. Eagles."

149

The nurse paused.

"She was admitted on Monday evening," said my mother helpfully.

"That's right," said the nurse. "Are you. . . ? Do you mind if I ask who you are?"

"Of course not," smiled my mother. "I'm Mrs. O'Leary. Her housekeeper. I brought her in."

"Mrs. Eagles isn't allowed visitors," the nurse said, softly.

"But when I phoned I was told that we could see her," said my mother surprised.

"The receptionist must've made a mistake," said the nurse. My mother looked suspicious.

"That's funny," she said. "Because Mrs. Turbett, she's a neighbor, saw Mrs. Eagles only yesterday."

"No visitors, I'm afraid," said the nurse briskly.

My mother didn't believe her, I could tell.

"What about her son?"

"Well, naturally," said the nurse. "Close relatives are allowed in for a short time."

I looked at the carnations.

"What about these?" I said.

"Take them home," said the nurse smiling down at me. "They'll look pretty in your bedroom, won't they?" She looked across at my mother. "I'm sorry. Excuse me."

My mother watched her retreating back thoughtfully.

"That's very strange indeed," she said.

All the way home in the bus, she was silent. Scowling. Angry at not being allowed to see Mrs. Eagles. When I asked her what I should do with the carnations, she shrugged and said to throw them out the window. I knew she didn't mean it so I hung onto them and when we got home, I put them in a vase on the dining-room table. They looked pretty. Coming out of the bedroom, my mother's gaze fell on them and without a word, she ripped them out of the vase. Marching through the back door, she lifted the lid and hurled them into the trash bag. She'd meant what she'd said after all.

Mr. and Mrs. McLean and Linda came to visit us soon after our visit to the hospital. They arrived at precisely two in the afternoon after phoning to see that it was convenient. A knock sounded on the front door and there they were in a prim little cluster, tidy in their best visiting clothes. Even though it was a scorching day, Mrs. McLean wore stockings. Her face was powdered and pointed, nostrils pinched as though the sight of us produced an unpleasant odor. Linda, in a trendy denim sunfrock and wooden clogs, had her hair tied back. I felt conspicuously grubby in my shorts and bare feet, as their neat pairs of eyes roved over me. They sat in orderly fashion, uncomfortably on their chairs, hands folded like monks' hands.

My mother seemed pleased to see them. Any form of social contact was better than nothing, it appeared, for she smiled and pattered out a lot of small talk about the weather, gardening and the terrible price of groceries. I sat gruffly on a dining chair, lolling with my legs apart. My mother paused in her conversation to tell me to 'sit up, dear' and the McLeans nodded their approval. It was the first glimpse of affability I'd seen so far.

Linda and I had said nothing to each other after they arrived, but she kept giving me surreptitious glances from under her eyebrows and shrugging messages to say that this had nothing to do with her.

The McLeans remained distant and my mother's friendly overtures dwindled and died. She went quickly to make tea while we sat in desultory silence, the odd remark melting into oblivion before it had a chance to come alive. Finally, after cups and cake had been passed around it came out—their interpretations of our visit to Mrs. Eagles's house. It was fairly accurate, ending with the letter of apology they'd sent to the hospital being returned unopened.

"I phoned to get the exact address, too," Mrs. McLean said, careful not to thaw out too much.

"She wouldn't accept it," he said.

"Linda was extremely hurt, weren't you, pet?"

Linda squirmed and said, "Aw, mum, shut up."

My mother told the story of our visit to the hospital. Everyone tich-tiched and we lapsed into silence.

"We've spoken to their teacher," Mr. McLean said at last. He dry coughed into his hand and eyed my mother's ankles. "He thinks they're a bad influence on each other."

I chewed the corner of my little fingernail, watching him sideways, wondering about the tension in his jaw and why he wouldn't look my mother in the face.

"He feels they should be separated," he said.

"It's all right for Harper," Mrs. McLean chipped in, eyes flowing over me like cleaning fluid. "She can cope if she wants to though it seems she prefers to muck about. But it's not fair on the ones who want to work. Is it Lindy?"

Linda glared at her mother. We grinned at each other.

My mother said, "Oh?" and settled more firmly in her chair.

"And then there was that spot of trouble at Mrs. Eagles's," Mr. McLean said.

His eyes roved over my mother's legs which were brown and wound around each other. I imagined that his hands were sweaty.

"They'd been drinking, you know," he said.

My mother nodded that she knew.

"Linda's never touched a drop of alcohol in her life before that."

My mother said that I wasn't exactly a hardened drinker.

Disapproving looks.

"What about that film, dear," Mrs. McLean prodded her husband. "Remember? Harper's birthday?"

I became suddenly alert. I was being threatened.

"What about the film?" said my mother. "It was quite suitable for their age."

"Remember what Linda told us? You know. She was that upset," Mrs. McLean prompted.

But he'd found something fascinating on the toe of my mother's sandle. His eyes were riveted there.

"Mum, you shut up," Linda said.

"Yes you were, dear. You cried and cried," Mrs. McLean said.

"You mean bitch," Linda said. "You promised you wouldn't say anything."

"I haven't said anything," said her mother.

She'd aroused my mother's curiosity though, and sat back, smug, satisfied.

"We thought we'd talk all this over with you," she smiled, "and see what you thought about keeping these two apart?"

Linda raised her shoulders at me in apology.

"It's vacation," said my mother. "They won't see much of each other anyway."

"That's true," laughed Mr. McLean, eyes on the V that her slacks made at her crotch.

"Especially as we're going away on Monday," his wife said.

"That should keep them apart," he said, and I wondered whether he was talking about us or my mother's legs.

"In the meantime, we'll hope they grow up a bit," said my mother.

Everyone tittered at the thought of us growing up. There was a flutter as tea cups were collected, crumbs swept from laps and the McLeans rose to leave. As I watched them clicking down the drive, I thought that I'd much rather live the way I did than have parents like Linda's.

My mother's voice jerked me out of my observations.

"What happened when you went to that film?" she said.

I went hot all over. Thank goodness I had my back turned.

"I haven't a clue," I said. "It was a pretty sad film. Linda freaked out at the end. You know, cried a lot. I can't think of anything else that happened."

"Strange to make a fuss about that," she said.

"The McLeans are strange people," I said, and she laughed.

It's boring now that Linda and I have been separated. I've got nothing to do. My mother's over at the big house giving it a last doing over as we're going away on vacation tomorrow. She thought it would be a good idea to take them now, while Mrs. Eagles is in the hospital. They told us that she wouldn't be coming home for at least another two weeks so we have plenty of time.

I'd offer to help with the cleaning but I don't want to go into the big house again. My mother understands.

I wander around to the front where Mr. Turbett is at his inevitable weeding. Ignores me all the time now. Just glares and shakes his head if he can't avoid my existence.

"Hello, Mr. Turbett," I say.

His head moves imperceptibly downwards. He's pretending that he hasn't seen me. As I scuff across the lawn, I feel like hurling armfuls of his weeds and yelling rude words at him. Instead, I walk toward the gate.

They blame me, the Turbetts. Think it was all my fault even though my mother explains that Mrs. Eagles would have had the stroke anyway. We both felt their disbelief. Just stood there shuffling, they did, not looking directly at us, muttering things like . . . "Is that so? "Well I never did!"

They've talked about me all over the neighborhood. I'm pretty sure because Mrs. Strong at the dairy isn't friendly any more. She's abrupt when I go in there now. She used to ask about my mother, and Mrs. Eagles, and how I was getting on at school. When I told my mother about Mrs. Strong, she said that I was being over-sensitive and imagining things. Shopkeepers are often too busy to gossip, she said. Anyway, other people had their problems, too.

I climb onto the wall, into my secret place.

My mother worries me. She's got that tight-lipped look and she sighs all the time. Surely we can't be getting ready to move again.

I was only three when we left my grandmother's. Everything seemed too much trouble for Granny, including me.

"Why should I look after your child while you go out to work?" she complained one day the moment my mother walked in the door. "Has it ever occurred to you that I might like a job? You're just like all the others, Kitty. Selfish."

"I pay you, don't I?" Kitty said.

"I'm too old to bring up another family," Granny said. "I did my best to bring you all up decently and look how you repay me."

"Good heavens! What's brought this on? Harper, have you been a naughty girl?"

Kitty cut a slice of bread, covered it liberally with jam and leaning against the bench bit into it. Granny sat at the table twirling her afternoon tea cup.

"I do everything for Harper, mum," Kitty said. "You don't have to do a thing except collect her from school and keep an eye on her until I get home."

"I want a life of my own," Granny said. "Without kids."

"What sort of a life do you think I'm having?" Kitty said.

"You can't blame me for that, Kitty. It's your own fault."

155

"I'm not blaming you. I'm not blaming anyone. I'm just telling you. It isn't much fun for me, either."

She took off her coat, slung it on the door knob and sat down opposite Granny.

"What's eating you all of a sudden?" she said.

"Gail and her five kids want to come here," said Granny. "That husband of hers isn't going to take them back and they've got nowhere to go."

"Christ!" said Kitty.

"How's everyone going to fit in?" moaned Granny, face saggy and old, "I haven't the room."

"Why do Gail and her brood have to come here? What's wrong with the flat they're in?"

"They've been evicted," said Granny. "Roy won't pay the rent."

"My God!" said Kitty. "I never did like that prick even before they were married."

"That's hardly the point," said Granny. "Your sister and her children have nowhere to live. There's six of them."

"And only two of me," Kitty said, eyes narrowing. "Is that what you're trying to say?"

Granny played with the cup again.

"I see," said Kitty, words ice-tipped. "Gail takes priority again. She always did, didn't she, mum?"

"At least she had a husband," muttered Granny.

"If you care to remember," said Kitty. "You invited me here to live. I didn't come of my own accord."

"I didn't intend that you should stay for ever. I just wanted to help out."

"And now your help's expired." Kitty's voice was tight with controlled anger. "Right. We'll go. Come on, Harper."

She grabbed her coat, bag, and me and stomped out of the

kitchen. The last I saw as I was dragged away was Granny's head leaning on her arms like a pumpkin.

We moved into a flat soon after with a woman called Hester who worked at the hospital with my mother. Hester had a little boy. She was a solo mother, too. Thin and whining, the boy, with a permanently runny nose. My mother used to grab him by the shoulder and squeeze his nose hard into toilet paper when Hester wasn't looking. He was being brought up the modern way, which meant that he was never yelled at or smacked and was always consulted about what he wanted to eat. When Hester was looking after me, I was consulted, too. I liked deciding what I would eat but it didn't suit the boy. Even though he got what he'd asked for, it never seemed to be what he'd expected. He would scream, flinging food all over the kitchen, dripping snot and tears down the front of his jersey.

Hester and my mother argued about money. It seemed that Hester never had any and was always promising to pay her share of the expenses which she never did. My mother got tired of paying for us and for Hester, too. We didn't stay long. Only three months and then we went to live with the Reverend Wilkins and his wife. That was when my mother gave up nursing and took up housekeeping. . . .

A car comes past. It's the McLeans. A bundle of beach gear looking like a fat corpse neatly wrapped in canvas is tied to the roof rack. Everything's as regimented as ever, I see, as they cruise slowly down our street. Mother and father in the front, Linda and Brent in the back, males on the right please, females on the left. No talking unless spoken to and the car dazzling high polish and care at the pedestrians.

I feel sorry for Linda. No wonder she's catty and nervous. No wonder she listens to and knows more dirty stories than anyone

157

else in the class. Reacting against her strict upbringing, my mother said. Still, I wouldn't want them to see me sitting here on a red brick wall at two-thirty on a Monday afternoon, half-hidden by foliage but with bare feet, grubby poking out. After all, a girl without a father who drinks alcohol and knows homosexuals. . . .

·16·

We went by bus to Hangunui. It took five hours. We'd never been there before and were disappointed at what we saw when we clambered out, dust-covered and stiff. Lonely it looked. Desolate, with a row of cottages strung like wooden beads along the metal road and in the camping ground—a cluster of Ministry of Works huts nestled down on the swampy foreshore. Hills, high and tangled in thick bush were close, seeming to press in on us so that deep blue shadows roamed over the ground.

The inside of our hut wasn't any better. Just four bunks running the length with a narrow chest of drawers in between and a table, a bench and two chairs at the other end. A naked bulb swung from the ceiling. Outside, a piece of wire stretched from the hut to a branch of a willow tree. The clothesline. The path to the wash house and cookhouse was springy with soggy marum grass. We discovered that the beach was a patch of mud, blancmange-like, and infested with crabs where it wasn't covered in the tangled heads of mangroves.

We felt a little dubious that first night lying in strange beds wondering what we'd find to do for ten days.

But as our holiday progressed, we enjoyed ourselves more and more. My mother bought two fishing lines and we spent endless hours on the old wharf, lines trailing in the salt-green water, offering hooks disguised in tantalizing pieces of pipi to any unwary fish that might be tempted. One day I caught a large silvery snapper, the only good catch either of us had and we barbecued it on the beach behind a heap of rocks. Delicious it was, the charcoaled flavor of newly caught fish.

We found a valley running up into the hills, bush cool, with a mountain stream winding through it. There we fished for eels, lying on the sun-warmed rocks, dangling lines into pools as dark as Indians' eyes. We ate sandwiches and read. Peaceful, so that all the problems of Rototui Street seemed to belong to another planet. My mother caught an eel. It flapped over the rocks, desperate, slimy and ugly. We shrieked and laughed because we didn't know what to do. Finally, she cut her line and the thing slid down the rock and back into the water. We played Scrabble and cards at night and listened to the radio. Once, we were invited to the owner of the camping ground's house to watch television but his wife was away and so we didn't go again.

My mother rang St. Luke's Hospital to see how Mrs. Eagles was. The matron who answered the phone told her to enjoy her vacation. Mrs. Eagles was just fine, she said.

Only one thing impaired our holiday and that happened on the last day. The owner's wife had quoted my mother off-season rates for the cabin. She had to pay twice as much as she had expected. She got a discount because of the mistake but it left us with little money to live on until she got paid again. And, she said, God knows when that will be.

So we jogged back to Roxton, a slight cloud hanging over us in spite of the good time we'd had. Grubby and tired from the long journey, we arrived in the city.

"Darn it," says my mother. "We've just missed one. The next one goes at. . . ."

Her finger runs down the glass pane covering the timetable. We're waiting for a local bus to take us home. I sit with my feet on my suitcase, wishing that a bus would never come so that I wouldn't have to face the emptiness of Mrs. Eagles's house again.

There's a sound of a horn from across the terminus and I look up to see Mrs. Strong from the dairy leaning out the window of her van, waving at us.

"Going home?" she booms.

We both nod and my mother says, "That's a stroke of luck."

Gathering our luggage we cross the road. I climb into the back and crouch among a stack of boxes. Mrs. Strong closes the doors on me. My mother settles herself into the front.

"Actually, I've just come into town to collect an order of sticking plaster," Mrs. Strong says. "We've been waiting for it for weeks."

"It seems an awful lot," I say, eyeing the boxes hemming me in.

"You'd be amazed how quickly we'll get through this lot," she says and starts the van. "Anyway, did you have a good vacation?"

"Great," says my mother. "We had a super time, didn't we, Harper?"

"Actually, I'm pleased to hear it," says Mrs. Strong as we shoot out into a stream of traffic. "Things don't look too good on the home front for you."

"Oh?" says my mother. "Why not?"

The van screeches to a stop at a set of lights so that I think we'll run into the trunk of the car in front of us. Mrs. Strong grinds the gears, swears and we leap forward.

"Gossip gets around, actually," she says, "and you'll probably think I'm gossiping for telling you this. . . ."

It's difficult for me to hear. The engine whines. There's a noise outside the van and Mrs. Strong has her back to me. I crawl forward and lean over between the two.

". . . Mrs. Turbett of course," she says. "Actually, she

says that Mr. Eagles is annoyed that you went away without telling him. Says that the house was left untended and what with all those valuable antiques, etc., anything could've happened. Most put out he is, actually."

"What a cheek," says my mother. "I've tried and tried to contact that man, and, anyway, Mrs. Turbett said she'd keep an eye on the place and try to contact Mr. Eagles for me."

Mrs. Strong chuckles.

"You'll learn," she says, "that no one who knows Mrs. Turbett would trust her with a rusty pin. Actually, she's the biggest gossip and troublemaker unhung."

"Really."

"Oh yes. She's dreadful. Do you know that she's still going on about how Harper nearly killed the old lady? Ridiculous, isn't it? But, actually, it's probably the most exciting thing that's happened to her since her wedding night."

I don't hear my mother's reply because Mrs. Strong bellows with laughter.

"Actually, jokes aside," she continues, "there've been some nasty rumors going around. Now I'm not one to gossip, but I think a person should know what he's up against, don't you?"

"Sometimes," says my mother cautiously. "But I really don't see that there's much to gossip about as far as we're concerned."

"Well, actually, there's been a lot of talk about Harper. . . ."

"Is that so? What, for example?"

My mother's suddenly alert.

"It's a hoot, actually. Harper being drunk. . . ."

"Good heavens," says my mother. "So what? Most kids try it out sooner or later."

"Of course. But it's where she got the stuff from that's so interesting, apparently."

My mother snorts.

"An. .d," says Mrs. Strong, dramatically, changing gear,

"there's talk that Harper is friendly with a crowd of homosexuals."

My mother's head jerks.

I just about faint.

"Now, where do people get such ideas?" Mrs. Strong goes on, unaware of the effect she's having on us. "I mean, a nice young girl like Harper! The story goes that she meets them in town and goes to bars and night-clubs and places like that with them."

"Good God!" explodes my mother.

I'm shocked. Linda. My best friend. There's a pain. Not a physical pain like a cut finger but a throb somewhere where I can't define. I want to cry.

We swirl out to face the on-coming traffic and for a moment I'm distracted. There's a cry of power from the engine and we all duck as we pass a car and skid onto our side of the road, narrowly missing a head-on collison with a car coming in the opposite direction.

"That was a close shave," Mrs. Strong says cheerily. "Did you know that Mrs. Eagles is due home tomorrow?"

My mother's reply floats away from me as the van is flung around a corner so that the tires screech and a heap of boxes land on top of me. I struggle to right them and myself.

"Actually, the son'll be in touch with you now, no doubt," says Mrs. Strong. "Do you know him? Arrogant young pup. Always was, even as a little boy."

She laughs self-consciously at having revealed a personal piece of herself, but my mother assures her that she's met Mr. Eagles and is inclined to agree.

We turn into Rototui Street and my heart sinks as I wonder what's in store for us. I wish that Mrs. Eagles was at home already because I feel sure that things would return to normal then and people would stop spreading vicious rumors about me.

"Here we are then," says Mrs. Strong, pulling up at our gate.

"Glad I met you, actually. Hope everything'll be okay. Let me know, won't you?"

We gather our belongings, thank her and assure her we'll let her know.

What, though?

The van hurtles off down the road and we're left standing on the footpath not wanting to go into our own home. It's the sad time of the day. In between light and darkness when the birds cry and the wind is still. Along the street, a few lights pinprick the dusk. Behind the lights people are snuggling up for the night. I'm aware of the devastation of my own world. My best friend Linda has deceived me. The Turbetts gossip about me. The whole neighborhood is wagging about my association with homosexuals. Lonely I feel. Like the end of the day.

"You'd better tell me," says my mother.

"What?"

"About Eric?"

She speaks flatly without anger or accusation.

"It's nothing much," I say knowing that my secret must be shared.

I hope she'll understand that I wasn't deliberately deceiving her but that my last meeting with him is something valuable which I don't want destroyed by any judgment she might pass. "Come on," she says. "Split."

I look at the street and draw circles in the gravel with my toe.

"We met him at the pictures. Linda and I. He talked to me, that's all, and Linda blew her mind. Freaked out. Thought it was disgusting. She must've told her mother."

"So that's it," says my mother. "I thought there was something more than just a sad picture."

I'm crying softly. She puts her arms around me and pushes my head onto her shoulder.

164

"Harper, I'm sorry, love. You're too young to be exposed to all this narrow-minded gossip. I promise that one day we'll have a proper home away from all these people who think that the way they live is the only way." She strokes my hair. "I promise. We'll have a place of our own with a huge garden and you can have a dog and a cat. Even birds if you like. I don't mind. Somewhere where you can have your friends to stay and a record player and we might even buy a little car if we can afford one. . . ."

She talks on, her voice muffled in my hair.

How can I tell her that that's not what I want? That I want to rewind the film and start again. I want to sit on the wall and listen to Diana talking about her boyfriend. I want to walk home with Barry and kiss him behind the macracarpa trees in the park. I want to eat Mrs. Turbett's cold meals and giggle with Linda. I want Mrs. Eagles to beckon me with her fat old fingers and to smile so that her pale eyes go watery. How can I tell her that I want to walk around the side of the big house after school and to see her waving at me from the kitchen window? That I want to sit on the doorway, chatting, eating raw carrot while she cooks our dinner. I don't want to go anywhere else. I don't want to shift again.

I pull away from her. We're on the sidewalk. Someone might see us.

"That'll be great," I say, sniffing, picking up a suitcase. "You're not mad at me?"

"Of course not," she says. "It's just a jolly shame that those McLeans are so bloody narrow-minded."

We struggle up the driveway. There's a strange car parked outside the garage.

"Who on earth can that be?" says my mother, frowning.

We go around the side of the house and see that there's a light on in our living room. I'm suddenly afraid and filled with anger.

165

Someone else is living in our house. But when we walk in, we find Mr. Eagles comfortably sprawled in an easy chair reading my copy of *Jonathan Livingston Seagull*. He rises languidly and looks at us with a polite but slightly insolent expression on his face.

My mother's furious. I can tell by the square set of her shoulders.

"Who gave you permission to walk in here?"

She starts right off, attacking.

"Mrs. Turbett said you'd be back this evening," he says. "I didn't think you'd mind."

"Well I do," snaps my mother and she walks straight past him and through to the bedroom.

I stand there gaping stupidly, ashamed of my mother's rudeness but admiring her courage at the same time. I don't know whether to follow her or to try to placate Mr. Eagles who is standing glowering at the bedroom door which has been slammed emphatically in his face. She solves my dilemma.

"Harper, bring that other suitcase in here," she calls.

Obediently I pick up the suitcase, say 'excuse me' to Mr. Eagles and go into the bedroom.

"What're we going to do?" I say in a panicky whisper.

"Nothing," she says. "Just carry on as though he isn't here."

She's unpacking, throwing dirty clothes into a pile on the floor, hanging the clean in the wardrobe. There's a coughing sound from the living room.

"Why don't you go and have a shower? Get ready for bed?" she says.

"I can't have a shower with him in the house," I say shocked.

She looks at me, puzzled, then laughs and hugs me.

"Thank God I've got you," she says.

I'm the puzzled one now. I'm about to tell her that she'd be better off without me when Mr. Eagles calls.

"Mrs. O'Leary I must speak to you. It's important."

"What about?"

My mother sounds gruff. Insolent.

"Mrs. Eagles. My mother."

She goes to the bedroom door. I stand behind her looking over her shoulder.

"I wouldn't have intruded except that this is important," he says, striding up and down. "As yet you won't know, but my mother is due out of the hospital tomorrow." He pauses and looks from under his eyebrows to make sure that we realize the importance of his words. "I'll be bringing her home at two o'clock. My wife and I will be moving in with her, as she's no longer capable of living on her own and. . . ."

"But I can look after . . ." interrupts my mother.

He raises his hand and his voice.

"Your services will no longer be required," he says.

Ugly pause.

"I see," says my mother, swallowing. "So you're giving me notice."

"It would appear so," he says, studying the highly polished tip of his shoe.

"I presume we have two weeks to find other accommodation?"

Her voice is cold steel.

He looks at her squarely for a few seconds.

"No, Mrs. O'Leary. You have until two o'clock tomorrow afternoon to vacate these premises. My mother must, on no account, see either you or your daughter. She is badly incapacitated as a result of your daughter's delinquent behavior and. . . ."

"You can't do that," shrieks my mother, out of control. "It's illegal."

"But I can," he says, calmly holding up his fingers to count

167

my mother's mistakes. "I haven't been able to contact you for the last fortnight. You've been away, remember. I consider you quite unsuitable as a housekeeper. You went away leaving this house empty. It could've been burglarized. You didn't even bother to let me know you were going. I consider that quite irresponsible."

"That's not true," says my mother. "You know damned well it isn't. I'd been trying to get in touch with you for weeks and finally I had to ask Mrs. Turbett to tell you we were away. Anyway, nothing's happened to the house."

"That's hardly the point."

My mother gulps. She tries another tactic.

"You're lying," she screeches. "You haven't been trying to contact me. You've been away."

"I can use a telephone, Mrs. O'Leary. Even on vacation."

"You're not my employer," says my mother, desperate now. "Mrs. Eagles is."

He holds up his hand.

"Mrs. O'Leary, my mother is no longer capable of making decisions. I must make them for her."

My mother stiffens.

"We're not moving," she says. "I want the proper amount of notice. I'm not budging until I get it. I'll see a lawyer."

"That would do you no good," he says in a patronizing, slightly bored voice. "I am a lawyer and I know precisely what is legal and what isn't."

"You're an importer," says my mother.

"I did law before I took over my father's business," he says.

Collapses, my mother does. Inwardly. Her shoulders sag; and shudders, like unreleased sobs, run up her back. But with her inner strength, her tenacity and stubborn pride which has enabled her to survive, she draws herself up. Rage takes over.

"Get out! Get out of here or I'll have you up for trespassing," she yells and throws my slipper which she's been holding.

168

He ducks but too late. The slipper hits the side of his face. His eyes widen with astonishment and he rubs his cheek. He's unsure now and tries to placate my mother.

"Please try and understand, Mrs. O'Leary. My mother's an old lady. She can't take too many upsets at her stage of life."

"Don't try and soft-soap me," snarls my mother. "You've been listening to that gossipy old bitch down the road."

He looks puzzled.

"I'm sorry. I don't know what you're talking about."

"Mrs. Turbett. It's her word against mine."

He gives an exaggerated sigh. He's finding my mother far more difficult than he anticipated.

"I've known the Turbetts a long time," he says as though speaking to a child. "Since I was a boy, in fact. And, yes, I find them most reliable. Decent reliable people."

"I see. And we're not?"

"You're not suitable for this job. You have a daughter who, from reports I've heard, needs a great deal of firm discipline. You can't give her that and care for an invalid, too. Surely your daughter's welfare is important to you?"

"How dare you," yells my mother. "That's none of your bloody business."

He's standing, hands behind his back, bouncing up and down on his toes, prosecutor, judge and jury condemning us to the streets and uncertainty.

He shrugs.

"That's the way it is, Mrs. O'Leary."

"You arrogant bastard," snarls my mother softly.

Ignoring that remark, he takes a wallet from the inside pocket of his jacket.

"You have three weeks wages due, I believe," he says and fingers a slim pile of blue, ten-dollar notes.

"Three weeks?" screams my mother. "I haven't been paid in five."

"Three weeks only," he says emphatically. "Your employment ended two weeks ago. But I'll add another ten for any inconvenience this may cause. That should be satisfactory, I think."

He licks his fingers and separates the notes slowly.

My mother is choking with rage.

"How the hell . . . ? How on earth . . . ?" She sounds close to tears. "How are we supposed to survive on that?" she shrieks.

"I don't know, Mrs. O'Leary," he says tiredly. "I really don't know."

He puts the notes down on the table and goes quietly out the door.

·17·

It is terrible packing. We have so little time and so many possessions. Our home is chaos and I can't stop crying. My mother was sympathetic, at first, but now she's impatient with me.

"Pull yourself together, Harper," she says. "It isn't the end of the world. God knows we've done it often enough. You should be uséd to it by now."

She has smudges under her eyes. Purple, like the juice from damson plums. She didn't sleep much, she said. Didn't say that she'd worried the night away.

Our things come pouring out of cupboards and drawers, and into suitcases. All the time she bosses. Do this, Do that. Put this over there. Get the things out of the bathroom cupboard, the hot-water cupboard, off the bookshelves.

I say that we shouldn't clean up, that we should leave the dust, the undefrosted fridge and the heaps of rubbish.

"Let those shitty Eagles do it," I sniff.

But she's determined to leave the place clean so we scrub and polish, searching out gray balls of fluff lurking in corners and under furniture, chasing away film from the skirtings, and cobwebs from the ceilings. Resentful, I feel, as I wipe window sills and ledges with a damp cloth.

"I won't have them saying around the neighborhood that we didn't leave the place as we found it," she says, down on her knees, scrubbing.

"They'll say it anyway," I say.

It takes a long time, packing, even though we've had lots of practice. We're not ready to leave until twenty to two. Rushing, as we've cut things a bit fine.

The taxi arrives, at last, backing up to our door and we pile things in, pile things in. There's only a space as wide as a shoe box left on the back seat for me. I rest one buttock on the seat, the other is pressed against a suitcase and the driver slams the door. I know that I'll have to stay in this position for the whole journey. My mother is in the front, loaded with coats and parcels so that she's hardly visible. The driver says that it's illegal to take so much luggage, but that he'll take the risk because we seem like nice people, and he doesn't want to leave us in a jam.

Imagine if he'd refused, I think. We'd be left sitting on our doorstep with all our luggage for Mr. Eagles to find.

As we turn out of our street, I visualize the Eagles's posh Rover cruising into it from the other end and the thought makes me cry again, quietly, into a sodden tissue. No one came to wave us goodbye. They probably don't even know we've gone.

Buses lumber in and out of the station and there's an awful smell of exhaust fumes. Fumes seem to lie in invisible puddles, making it unpleasant to breathe. There's a continual stream of people along the platforms and I think how serious they all look as I munch my bag of potato chips. Lots of Henny Pennies with acorns about to drop on their heads.

I'm surrounded by luggage. It spews out over the platform so that people have to detour around it. But I don't care. I don't care about anything much at the moment. Drained I feel, as though someone has pulled the plug out on my emotions.

The end of summer and here I am again, one year later, one

year older, waiting almost exactly as I was this time last year, homeless and with possessions scattered in full public view. I hope no one I know comes past. It's so embarrassing I could die.

I pull my copy of *Film Review* up close to my face, pretending to read but really I'm hiding.

My mother went off, worried, purse jingling with nickels and dimes.

"Who're you going to ring up?" I asked.

"I don't know yet. I'll have to buy a paper," she said, concern wiping out any pretense that everything would be all right.

She said that I was to stay here and look after the luggage and that she wouldn't be long but she's been gone for ages.

Boredom makes me feel like doing something crazy. I could take my clothes off, dance naked along the platform and laugh at all the shocked faces. Instead, I empty the scraps from my bag onto the ground, and watch the sparrows, like little vacuum cleaners, pecking up my debris.

I told Mrs. Strong our news this morning when I went to the dairy for the milk. Later, she came to our house with some empty cartons. Crushed me, when she saw I was crying. Squeezed me so hard that I thought I'd be several centimeters taller by the time she let me go.

"You're a silly young rabbit, actually," she said in her husky voice. "Is this all you want out of life? This hut stuck in someone else's backyard and not even a proper place to bring your friends to?"

"No," I said, because that's what she wanted to hear.

"That's my girl," and she pressed me tight again.

She looked around the room and, without a word, began gathering up winter clothes to fold into a carton.

"Have you got somewhere to go?" she asked my mother.

173

My mother said, "No, not yet. But we'll be all right."

She didn't sound as though we'd be all right or look it either. Mrs. Strong eyed her thoughtfully then tich-tiched and folded another jersey.

"You mustn't think I'm trying to organize you," she said, "But you could go and stay in my brother's house for a few days. He's overseas. I don't know what he does with the key but I could find out. He wouldn't mind in the least."

My mother said that no, really, she'd rather not.

"Well," said Mrs. Strong, "There are always those halfway houses. Actually, they're set up for women and children in a spot of trouble. There's a new one just opened, actually. Over in the highland suburbs. That'd do you for a day or two, wouldn't it?"

My mother said she supposed it would and Mrs. Strong, considering the problem solved, went on flinging clothes capably into the carton. I saw the stubborn lines around my mother's mouth and knew that we'd sleep under a hedge before we accepted what she called common charity. But Mrs. Strong didn't know this about her.

Uncertainty gripped me again, causing an ache in my stomach. The sadness of leaving was heightened by the precariousness of our future. We worked in silence.

"One thing," Mrs. Strong said at last, trying to be cheerful, "you'll be okay for money with government aid. Actually, I believe you get quite a good whack these days."

She was tying a carton, stretching a piece of twine around its fat belly.

"There now," she said, patting it with satisfaction. "That should hold pretty well, actually."

She looked over and smiled at my mother.

"Is it really all that good?"

"What's that?" said my mother.

"The government aid."

"I don't know," said my mother, kneeling back, brushing the hair from her face. "I've never had it."

Astonishment on Mrs. Strong's face.

"But my dear girl, you're entitled to it," she said. "Actually, I was just saying to my Reg the other day that if there's one person who deserves it, it's you. All you have to do is to go and see those people at the Social Welfare Department. I don't know where it is, actually, but it'll be in the phone book."

"I know where it is," said my mother.

"Pop in there this afternoon," said Mrs. Strong. "They might even give you a little bit to go on with. I believe they do, sometimes."

Sure that she'd patched up another hole in our lives, she hummed as she dragged a carton over to the front door.

"I don't need any help from the state," said my mother. "I can manage on my own."

Mrs. Strong's eyes, mouth, whole face sagged. She was about to say something but shrugged instead and reached over for another empty carton. She found my mother's attitude too peculiar to cope with. I did, too.

Mrs. Strong was kind. She was trying to help. She was aware of our depression and was trying to bolster us. I wished my mother wouldn't be so churlish. So ungrateful.

We had some coffee, sitting on the floor among the boxes, and then Mrs. Strong said she'd have to go. She was sorry she couldn't drive us anywhere, she said, but her husband needed the van and she'd have to look after the shop. She gave me a present. An address book. She'd already put hers in so that I'd remember to keep in touch.

I was sorry to see her go.

Twenty-five minutes past four by the bus station clock and here she comes, clicking along the platform. There's something buoyant about her step and the resentment of the long wait drifts away.

"Hello, darling," she says, swathed in smiles and sunlight. "Sorry I've been so long. Here, I've brought you something nice to eat."

She holds out a white paper bag. Two chelsea buns with pink icing and raisins like teddy bear's eyes protruding from the dough.

I lick the icing on one and say, "Where've you been? What took you so long? How did you get on?"

"All fixed up," she says and laughs. "But we've got to hurry. We've got a train to catch."

I look at her in admiration. I don't know how she does it. A few hours ago, we were destitute and almost out of our minds with worry. She disappears for a while and comes back again organized. Incredible, she is.

"Tell me," I say. "Where're we going?"

She begins gathering up pieces of luggage, stalling, teasing me, grinning.

"You'll see," she says

I feel frustrated.

"Don't be so mean. Tell me."

"Okay," she says. "Do you remember last year in that awful boarding house we met that nice man called Mr. Wilson? He had an art. . . ."

"Of course," I say. "You mean you rang up Mr. Wilson?"

"Yes. And he wants us to go and stay with him for a while. He's expecting us tonight. Isn't that great?"

We laugh and hug each other.

"Neat," I say. "Really neat. Are we going there? Honest?"

176

"Honest," says my mother. "But we'll have to hurry. The train leaves at four forty-five and we've got to find a taxi to get us to the station."

"Let's go," I say, grabbing at our possessions.

But, as I stagger across the taxi stand, I'm filled with apprehension. A terrible shyness comes over me and I don't want to go. What if Mr. Wilson thinks we're weird like everyone else does?

· 18 ·

"What're you doing? Is the rotary hoe broken again?" I say as I wander into the toolshed to find Mr. Wilson carefully handling pieces of the dismantled machine.

He straightens his back, arching, and sits on an upturned box. With an oily cloth, he wipes his hands in that ponderous manner which, I've learned, is characteristic of farmers. He blows the ash off his cigarette without removing it from his mouth.

"No, nothing the matter with it, Harper. I'm just taking the depth-control skid off."

"What's that?"

"This thing here."

He taps a thing that looks like a short ski and explains that it usually takes the weight off the rear of the machine, and regulates the depth to which the hoe blades can dig into the soil.

"With the skid on, the hoe can cut anything up to nine inches deep," he says and flings his cigarette butt onto the dirt floor, grinding it with his heavy boot. "But I'm taking it off now so that I can fit this joker here on instead."

As he speaks, he takes an enormous metal V from the bench, fits it onto the place where the skid had been and bolts it securely.

"Now we're ready to make furrows for the potatoes," he says.

"Kitty said would you come and have morning tea, now," I say. "She's made another one of those pineapple upside-down cakes."

Mr. Wilson grins.

"By golly," he says, "I do like the weekends with your mother doing all that baking. And having you around to give me a hand."

He slings an arm over my shoulder and we walk across the yard together, in through the back gate toward the house.

He makes me feel important telling me things and sometimes asking what I think. It's as though he and I run the market garden together.

Kitty calls: "Come on you two. The tea's been made for ages. It'll be cold if you don't hurry up."

After washing his hands at the outside tap, Mr. Wilson sits on the steps and takes his boots off. We go into the house, me in bare feet, he in his socks, and sit at the kitchen table. My mother pours the tea and Mr. Wilson takes a large slice of the pineapple cake, indicating with his eyes that he thinks it delicious.

She glows in his unspoken praise.

I gaze out the window at the navy-blue clouds sitting on the soft curve of the distant hills. Below, in the valley, a line of poplars has briefly turned yellow. But already the wind is sending the leaves skittering across the paddocks and I know that in a day or two the trees will be pale gray and barren. Near the house, the earth has been churned chocolate brown and soon Mr. Wilson will patiently run the rotary hoe over it to gouge grooves and ridges ready for planting. I think of all those potatoes spread out to green under the pine trees and how, this weekend, they'll be put to bed, the earth heaped over them to make rows of mountain ranges like the ones on the *papier mâché* relief we made in geography.

"Why do the potatoes have eyes?" I say.

Mr. Wilson chuckles.

"So they can see to grow," he says.

For a moment I almost believe him.

179

Kitty laughs and says that the eyes are the shoots, the place where the new plants start growing from.

She doesn't work at the weekends. Mr. Wilson said that she should be at home with me then, so she told the people who own 'Ridge Heights Motel', where she's a housemaid, that she could only work during the week. They accepted that because good staff are difficult to find in a small town like Ngaurimu.

Every morning, she peddles off on an old bicycle she bought, down the rough metal driveway, out onto the road, careering down the hill toward the bridge and out of sight. She goes so fast and seems so abandoned that sometimes I worry that she'll hit something and have an accident. Seems to enjoy it, though, that early morning ride, her hair streaming behind like streaks of golden syrup.

Mr. Wilson and I make our own breakfasts and clean up. Then I walk down the drive to catch the school bus and he goes out into his garden.

Strange, the way Kitty takes notice of Mr. Wilson. Usually it's the other way around. Kitty tells the men what to do and they do it. Quiet Mr. Wilson is. He suggests things. . . . 'I thought perhaps . . .' 'What do you think about . . . ?' Kitty becomes thoughtful, smiles and says that it's a good idea. I watch and think how clever he is. Diplomatic, and I like him for it.

"That was very nice indeed," he says, leaning back in his chair and lighting a cigarette.

Kitty says, "Have another cup?"

He raises his hand.

"No. That'll do for now. By golly, you'd turn me into a barrel in no time at all."

He chuckles, pats his stomach and goes out. Soon he appears with the rotary hoe in the paddock closest to the house. I sit at the kitchen window watching the blade bending the earth backwards so that it looks like cookie mixture coming out of a factory machine. Seagulls, landing behind him, contrast sharply with the dark color of the churned ground. Clouds of dust rise and my nostrils twitch as I imagine it tickling my face.

Behind me, Kitty fusses, taking a leg of lamb out of the freezer for tonight's dinner, rinsing the morning tea dishes, adding things to her shopping list, humming.

Five months we've been here, now, though we only intended to stay a fortnight at the most. But we fitted in, in a natural kind of way, after the first night when everyone felt awkward.

Mr. Wilson had gone to a lot of trouble that night, cooking us a big roast dinner and setting the table in the dining room, using his best cloth instead of using the kitchen and the formica-topped table. He'd showered before we arrived. I could tell because he had a freshly scrubbed look and there were dollops of soap behind his ears. He wore a white shirt and a tie and his good shoes instead of his comfortable paint-splattered slippers. It made the occasion seem special. It had an artificial air about it.

All evening he ran, with a tea-towel across his arm, from the lounge to the kitchen to check the food, and his face became beet red. The eyelid over his good eye drooped, making the artificial eye seem strangely wide and alert. My mother kept asking if there was anything we could do but he insisted that we 'sit and relax'. We would much rather have helped but we sat primly in the lounge with nothing to say to each other except to make empty remarks.

"It's a comfortable room."

181

"I like these red linen chair covers."

"Isn't that picture like the one we saw in the Art Gallery? Remember? That Sunday?"

Mr. Wilson would come and talk for a few minutes, perching on the arm of a chair. He said things like—"I hope you'll be comfortable" and "I'm a bachelor now that Mrs. Wilson's gone"—a remark that set my imagination on fire but it turned out, as he explained later to my mother, that she'd died six years ago after a long illness through which he'd nursed her.

All through dinner, Mr. Wilson apologized for the meal so that my mother and I ate far too much to prove how good it was. But the next morning he no longer considered us visitors. The pretense was over. We had breakfast in the kitchen and Mr. Wilson set us to work.

"You man the toaster, Harper," he said, "and don't burn the toast. That's all the bread we've got."

My mother said, "Here, let me cook the eggs. You set the table. You know where everything's kept."

Already she was feeling at home enough to be bossy.

And so, we slipped into a pleasant routine, one which Mr. Wilson seemed to welcome as much as we did. When the school term was about to begin and my mother made noises to indicate that we should be moving on, Mr. Wilson said that it was silly to unsettle me again and that we seemed to be getting along nicely, why didn't my mother enroll me at the local school? She did and the very next day she took the job at the motel. It seemed that our future, for the time being, was secure.

It is peaceful here, nestled into the side of the hills with the green-brown bush rising behind us and the valley spreading below. We look down on the township of Ngaurimu which sits on the flats like a cluster of mtachboxes.

It's hard to decide who Mr. Wilson prefers. Sometimes I

182

think it's me, sometimes my mother, and he's always careful the way he meters out his attention. We're still friends like when we first met. We have jokes together which my mother doesn't share but they have their adult jokes, too, which exclude me. I feel the twinge, then, the need to be alone with my mother. I become suspicious, afraid that something will happen to spoil what we have or that my mother will be taken away from me.

She says, "Come on, Harper, stop dreaming and set the table for lunch."

"What're we having?" I say.

"Soup. And bran muffins."

"Yuk," I say and she glares at me.

After lunch we carry the boxes of seed potatoes over to the paddock and start planting. We set the seeds about sixteen centimeters apart, careful not to break off the fragile green shoots. I work down the rows steadily, quickly getting into a rhythm but even though there's no sun and the wind is brisk, I find it hot work. At first, I thought my body rubber which bent to my will, but it soon turns wooden and I wait for the crackle of vertebrae as my back begins to ache. Every now and then, I have to straighten up, push my stomach muscles forward and rub the small of my back. I notice that Kitty straightens up often too, but Mr. Wilson seems not to notice the pain of continual bending.

Although the potato patch isn't large, it's late afternoon by the time we finish. Kitty and I go to the house to put the dinner on while Mr. Wilson takes the furrower to cover the rows so that the new seeds won't be exposed if there's a frost.

As we go toward the house, boots mud-caked, fingernails packed and dirty, I feel the sudden crispness of winter in my lungs. The sky is deep gray and tinged with the flames of autumn. From the orchard comes the self-important but querulous warble of a blackbird.

"God, I'm tired," says my mother. "I can't wait to have a shower and get clean."

I'm tired, too. A pleasant bone-aching tiredness and I think of hot water raining down on my body, the fire in the living room and clean hair falling over the collar of my dressing gown. Mr. Wilson's pipe. Blue smoke and tobacco smells. . . .

I'm only pretending to watch television. I'm watching them. There's something between them. They're sitting on the couch, Kitty with her legs bent and up, her elbow on the back, head resting in her hands. Mr. Wilson's reading the paper, choosing snippets to read aloud to her. She's too close to him, laughing that false laugh of hers. He seems relaxed and there's a new vitality in his body, an alertness which makes him look younger. They seem to be waiting for some secret sign, some sort of body langugage which only they can decipher.

"By golly," he says. "Listen to this," and Kitty leans imperceptibly closer to him. "It says, 'Nick Osborne, the motorcycle sidecar passenger who crashed during the round-the-streets *Grand Prix* at Handley yesterday, is progressing favorably in St. Martin's Hospital. He is believed to have a broken leg, broken pelvis and other injuries'." There's a crackle of paper. "A nice lad that, too. I used to live next door to the Osbornes when I had my farm down the Kipikipi. Young idiot, eh? The power of speed. These young jokers can't resist it."

"I hate to hear about young people smashing themselves up." says my mother.

Her fingers reach out and gently twine the hair at the nape of his neck. His head moves backwards to caress her touch. She withdraws. Silent communication has passed between them and my body goes stiff. I'm furious. My little finger finds its way to my mouth and my teeth pull viciously at the nail.

My mother looks up and says, "Harper, aren't you tired, love? You should be in bed."

"It's Saturday night and I'm watching the film," I say tersely, feeling tears forcing their way into my eyes. "Would you mind being quiet."

Glints in her eyes. Body taut. She's about to retaliate but then relaxes. I don't suppose she wants one of our verbal altercations tonight.

They return to the paper, ignoring me. I pretend to be absorbed in the program but I can see them out of the corner of my eye. He strokes her arm and she moves her foot so that her slipper rests on top of his. Disgusting, it is, grown-up people behaving like this. I hate to see it. Especially my own mother. Embarrassing, watching her being sloppy like those American filmstars in the old war movies we see on television. Mr. Wilson stretches and pats her knee. I'm filled with rage. I don't know how she can bear to have him touch her in that way as though he owns her.

"Time for a cup of tea," he says. "I'll put the kettle on."

They have one of those, 'I'll do it. No, I'll do it' conversations. Under my breath, I mimic them, my face screwing up into the contempt I feel. To me, they're behaving like a stupid pair of five-year-olds. He loses. At least, that's what I think because he's committed to making us all tea.

"Why don't you make it, Harper?" says my mother and immediately my whole being is riveted to the television set. I pretend not to have heard.

"Harper?"

Voice raised.

No way will I leave them alone together. I know that's what they want but I'm not going to do it.

185

"Sh-sh" I say. "Can't you see I'm watching this?"

Mr. Wilson says, "Leave her. She worked hard this afternoon. I'm making it. Would you like one, too, Harper?"

I shrug, not looking at him. Being rude, and I know it but I don't care.

"What does that mean?"

A sharp note like jagged glass in my mother's voice.

Glaring at her, I say, "It means yes. Don't you even know that yet?"

"Three for tea," says Mr. Wilson and goes out.

"You must be very tired, Harper," my mother starts in the moment he's out of the room. "I hope we're not going to have to put up with another bout of your bad temper. I really don't know why you behave like this. Mr. Wilson is so good to you."

"And to you, don't forget," I say, unable to keep the resentment out of my voice.

She reads my eyes, the tone of my voice and backs down a little.

"To us both. We're lucky to be here and your behavior really isn't repaying him," she says more quietly.

"What've I done?" I say. "You're always accusing me. Of all sorts of things."

"There's no need to shout," she says and picks up the paper.

"Well? Go on. What've I done now?" I demand, feeling braver with the paper between us.

"Oh, for goodness sake," she says. "Just try and be a little more pleasant, will you?"

I should be quiet now. Before she loses her temper. But I hate what's going on between them. The way I'm left out.

"You're pleasant enough for both of us," I sneer.

She looks at me, frowning.

"What do you mean by that, young lady?"

"You know perfectly well what I mean. I've seen you. Slopping all over him. Yuk!"

There's silence. The prologue to one of our slanging matches. It's long and quiet enough for me to notice that there's the drumming of rain on the roof and I think that the potatoes will be free from frost tonight. From the kitchen comes the clatter of cups on saucers. I can see from the heave of her chest that she's gathered her resources and is ready for battle. But the door opens and Mr. Wilson comes in carrying a tray. Immediately, she's on her feet pulling a side table over near the couch, making appreciative noises to tell him how good he is.

"That was well timed," he says, glancing at the box. "I like a good comedy."

We have supper. I feel so lonely that I'm cold even though the room is warm and I'm closest to the fire. I watch their contentment, a long way outside of it and think about my own father. It's ages since I've seen him. I don't suppose he knows where I am. He didn't send me anything for my birthday this year.

Doggedly, I sit it out until the night's programs are over and Mr. Wilson turns off the set. We go to bed. He to his room, she to ours.

· 19 ·

Friday and we've caught the train into Roxton. Just Kitty and I. I had to wear mufti to school and to get out early because the only train for town leaves at five past three. My mother wrote a note asking permission and I met her at the station. The journey takes an hour.

It's late afternoon when we get there and drizzling. The street lights are on—orange splodges spreading like candle wax on the streets. There's a hissing sound as car tires displace water, and their lights draw stripes on the wet roads.

The main street has the atmosphere of a carnival. Friday night shopping always make me think this. There are so many shapes and colors filtering past. People are dressed casually or in their best, loitering, gossiping, hurrying, relaxed or tense, and they look as though they've donned fancy dress and are taking part in a massive Mardi Gras. Excitement inside me as we join the procession.

First we go to Woolworth's. Kitty buys a bag of hard jubes and we eat them as we browse, jostling and being jostled by other shoppers. On a tray, I see some pretty silver bracelets with clusters of beads dripping like soap bubbles. I hold one up, admiring it, wanting to buy it. Kitty and I have a brief discussion, and, finally, she gives in. I take a long time choosing the one I want. She buys a pair of socks for Mr. Wilson. They're dark bown and conservative.

Out on the street again, she threads her arm through mine

so that she won't lose me and we wander up the street feeling the old closeness that existed between us during the earlier part of our stay at Mrs. Eagles's place. We window gaze, admiring the new spring fashions, choosing ourlandish garments for each other and dying with laughter. The game becomes more and more ridiculous until she tires of it.

"Come on," she says. "I've got a million things to do. Let's go over to Allenby's and get some curtain material for the kitchen."

Quiet it is in Allenby's. A staid, cool shop where the salesmen will ponder with the customer for as long as he or she wishes. And Kitty dithers. Bored by her lack of decision, I wander off among the suites and beds.

"Hi, Harper."

I swing around to find Tony Caldwell, Diana Pardon's boyfriend standing there. I'd forgotten that he worked at Allenby's. He's grinning, face blond-thatched, seeming pleased to see me.

"How're things?" he says, hands clasped behind his back in that departmental-manager fashion.

"Hi, Tony. How're you?"

We tell each other that we're both okay and then stand awkwardly, smiling.

"This's a funny place to meet you," he says. "Are you setting up house or something?"

I nod my head in the direction of the curtaining department.

"My mother's buying some material. How's Di? I mean. . . ."

Hot, my face. Perhaps he's not friendly with Di anymore and will think me naive or tactless. He's tall and good looking. I wouldn't want him to think that.

"She's fine. She's at Varsity this year," he says with a note of pride in his voice that tells me they're still together and I haven't said the wrong thing. "She likes it okay, too, though she didn't think she would to start with. Some pretty way-out people there."

I say that that's great and ask about the other members of her family. He tells me. Mr. Pardon was hit on the side of the head with a golf ball and had delayed concussion. Nicholas is at St. Paul's this year. He adds with a touch of delight in his voice that they'll straighten out the little bugger. Mrs. Pardon has had a trip to Fiji and the cat's had another litter. Apart from that they're just the same.

"Where're you living now?" Tony says.

A twinge of embarrassment and I look at the floor. He reaches out emotionally to comfort me. A sympathetic gesture without touch.

"Out at Ngaurimu," I say. "We've come into town to do some shopping."

"Do you like it?"

I nod.

"Yes. It's quite good. The school's a bit rough. You know, some kids on drugs and all that but we've got this really neat art teacher who takes us on trips to the beach and places like that to collect things. You know. Driftwood and rocks and things. It's neat fun."

He says, "Hey! Did you hear about the uproar when your old landlady came back from hospital?"

I'm immediately puzzled, defensive. What's he talking about?

"Don't tell me you've forgotten already?" he says. "Mrs. Eagles."

"No," I say. "I haven't heard anything."

He moves closer with that confidential 'I've-got-a-juicy-bit-of-gossip-to-tell' expression and I want to run.

"She was so angry when she found you'd left she nearly had another stroke, the poor old girl," he says with a chuckle.

"It wasn't our fault," I say.

190

"I know that. That's why she nearly flipped her lid. She didn't think it was your fault either and she thought you'd still be there. It was that bastard of a son of hers who evicted you off his own bat. She didn't know anything about it."

I stared at him. Speechless.

"Don't you see?" he says waving his hands at me as though I'm stupid. "It was her son who did it. Mrs. Eagles didn't want you to leave."

Incredible, to hear this after so long. I visualize the large old lady with the cracked clay face. Her pudgy finger beckons me and her precise voice asks, 'Are you a good child? Do you like jewelry?' I feel grateful that she doesn't blame me.

But I say nonchalantly even though secretly I'm pleased and flattered, "Oh well! It's too late now. We're living in such a neat place we wouldn't come back anyway. Even if they did ask us."

"It's true though," he says. "Honest. Ask Mrs. Pardon if you like. She goes and sits with Mrs. Eagles sometimes 'cause the old girl's bed-ridden."

I grin in spite of a desire to appear unimpressed. Warmth rises from my toes like a barometer in the summertime.

"Mrs. Pardon said," Tony goes on, "that she wishes she knew how to get in touch with you. Shall I tell her?"

"It's no use," I say, though in my mind I see our future crystallizing into a wealthy existence in the Eagles mansion.

Tony shrugs. "Please yourself," he says.

He slaps the top of my arm.

"Hey! Here's old Bandy Legs back. It's my tea break. See you, Harper."

He strides off through a curtained doorway.

I'm ecstatic. I want to sing and shout. I feel that I'm flying, kite-like, dipping and swirling, humming to the accompaniment of the wind. Just wait until Kitty hears this.

I find her among the imported china.

"There you are," I say. "I've got. . . ."

191

"I've been looking for you everywhere," she says. "Where've you been?"

"I've got something terrifically fabulous to tell you," I say, dancing around her. "I met. . . ."

She jams things into her shopping basket.

"Come on," she says.

She heads for the door.

"Tony Caldwell," I say prancing behind her.

"That's nice," she throws over her shouder.

"And he said. . . ."

I lose her. By the time I've maneuvered through a crowd of people she's made the door and is holding it open impatiently.

"Hurry up," she says. "The seed place closes at seven."

"Tony said that. . . ."

"Tell me later. It'll keep."

She strides off, determinedly. Kitty knowing where she's going and me trotting along behind thinking how strange it is that mothers never have time to listen when there's something important to tell them. Mine isn't unique. I know that from my friends.

Porter Grain and Seed Merchants is up a side street which after the main street is dimly lit. As we traipse toward it, we pass Eric's light-fitting showroom, a square of sunshine in the dark street. It glitters with hanging lights, strange shapes dangling from the ceiling like mobiles. I slow my pace to stare in but Kitty forges ahead, eyes firmly on the sidewalk. There's a man with a bald head and glasses behind the counter, thumbing through a book. Probably an invoice book, I think.

For the first time, I'm aware of all the ghosts this city holds for me. Too much of my past, like pockets of mist, lurk in unexpected places.

I wonder what I would do or say if Eric stepped out and we came face to face. I know it's impossible because he never comes

192

here. It's one of his smaller concerns, inherited from his father and run by a manager. But I think about it. Whether the ambivalent feelings I've recently been having would change on seeing him. Would I hate or love him? Would he still be Eric or would he have taken on some new guise? I feel that he's a Dr. Jekyll and Mr. Hyde character, some textured craggy form, ugly and unfathomable one moment, the charming, familiar Eric of my past the next. I'm awfully mixed up about him. There is only one sure thing and that is that I do want to see him again.

By the time I catch up to Kitty, she's ordered Mr. Wilson's seeds.

We go hunting for shoes. There's a lot on my mind and I can't concentrate properly. Keep saying that the shoes are okay and that I like every pair I try on. Kitty's getting tight around the mouth and the shop assistant is tapping her forearm with the shoehorn. It's getting on for eight-thirty and time we were heading for the station. I've got to make a decision. I close my eyes and stab.

"These ones," I say.

"Are they comfortable? Do they fit properly?" says my mother. "Stand up and walk around in them."

I oblige, clonking up and down the showroom.

"They're neat," I say.

"Can you wear them with all your clothes? Think, Harper."

Again I oblige, I gaze at the door saying, "Uhm" but can't visualize one garment in my wardrobe.

"Yes. They'll go with almost everything," I say.

Kitty smiles relief.

"We'll take them," she says.

At the station we buy cups of tea and meat pies. At last I can tell Kitty my news.

193

She's silent. As stunned as I was.

"I'm terribly pleased," she says at last. "I really am."

"We could go back there," I say to test her out.

She shakes her head.

"Things are never the same when you go back."

"But still . . . it'd be nice to live there again. In our own little house."

She looks at me and laughs.

"Darling, what about Mr. Eagles? How would you like him living next door?"

"Yuk!" I say.

I nibble my pie, avoiding the yellow-green peas.

"Mrs. Eagles'd tell him to leave," I say. "I bet she would. If we went back."

"Her own son?" says my mother.

"We could ask. Find out if she would."

Kitty stirs her tea. Thoughtfully.

"She was a dear old lady. I'd grown so fond of her. I wonder, if we wrote to her, whether she'd get the letter?"

"We could try," I say.

"We'll do that," she says. She smiles that dreamy smile. "As soon as we get home."

Home? I feel the old resentment rising. It was good, this evening, just Kitty and me. Like old times. But now we've got to go back to Mr. Wilson's place. To divide ourselves a bit further to accommodate him.

"I'd really like to go back to Mrs. Eagles's," I say.

"Come on," she says. "Time to go. You carry your shoes and this."

She seems eager. She doesn't really care about Mrs. Eagles. Or me.

At Ngaurimu Station, Mr. Wilson is there to meet us. He walked down as he isn't allowed to drive with only one good eye.

194

As we force a passage through the darkness, my mother chatters about what we did, how she ordered the seeds and bought me shoes.

He says, "You've both had a good time then? Pleased with your shoes, Harper?"

I say that they're okay, I suppose.

I'm sure that they're walking close together and as we pass under a street light, I see that her arm is linked in his. He notices me looking and reaches out to join me to them but I pull away.

Swinging around a lamp post, I sing:

Round and round the mulberry bush,
Kitty found a chair.
But when she went to sit on it
She crashed
Because it wasn't there.

My mother says, "Don't be silly, Harper."

I can't understand myself, why I'm doing it.

They walk on. Ignoring me. That makes me angry. I scuff in the gutter, kicking up cushions of damp leaves. I chant:

'There were two lovers
Aho ahay.
In the seed shed one day they lay.
He said, Allow me, allow me, I pray.
She said, You may oh you may.'

My mother stops and turns around. I can't see the expression on her face but her voice tells me she's not amused.

"Get out of the gutter at once and stop being so childish," she says.

She catches up with Mr. Wilson and they stroll ahead of me.

Ashamed I feel. Foolish. Tear-pricking around the eyes.

I mutter, "Shut up you silly old bitch," and continue to scuff in the gutter.

195

·20·

It's still dark. I hug my coat around me, pulling the collar up over my ears. I stamp my feet but quietly. Don't want to attract attention. There are people here who will recognize me. Mrs. Millar for example. She knows who I am and I know her even though we've never spoken. I know that she goes into the city every morning to work in a sandwich bar. And there's Mr. Lochore sitting in the shelter, huddled, with his hands tucked into his armpits. He's friendly with Mr. Wilson so he must know who I am. It's too dark to recognize the other people, two of them standing out of the light, crouched concrete figures. Solitary, we are. Separate, like fence posts with our common destination the wire that joins us.

I wonder which will arrive first, the train or the dawn. It's one of those overcast mornings, sludgy with mist and drizzle so there won't be a proper dawn. Just a lightening of the grayness.

I dread the moment when the light comes and wish the train would hurry. I'd be vulnerable, exposed to the early morning commuters of Ngaurimu. Perhaps someone would strike up a conversation and ask why I'm here. The thought makes me restless and I peer into the black tunnel where the railway tracks should be. No balloon of light swells toward me.

It seemed a good idea last night but now I'm getting niggles of doubt. I'm thinking of all sorts of things I didn't consider before. How humiliating it would be if Kitty and Mr. Wilson had already missed me. They'd come storming onto the platform to take me home. My mother would make a scene in front of all these people. She'd abuse me in a loud voice. She might even slap me if she were angry enough. I'd die of embarrassment.

What if no one wants to recognize me when I get there? They might be rude and slam the door in my face. Or call the police. But they won't. Not when I tell them.

Touching my school case with the calf of my leg, I feel comforted. Cunning, I've been, bringing only one small case and my school one besides. They won't suspect I've run away because all my belongings will be there except the few that I really care about—the turquoise brooch that Mrs. Eagles gave me, the brush and comb set that Kitty and Mr. Wilson gave me for my birthday, my pajamas and some clean underwear, the natural wool jersey that Kitty knitted me—all jammed into the case so that it's nearly bursting. Hid my school books in the toolshed under some sacks. It'll be ages before they find them. I've remembered my toothbrush and transistor but I've forgotten to bring a handkerchief.

The train is upon us before I realize. There's a burst of light and a rushing sound as it sweeps into the station. I feel the platform moving. The dawn's here, too. Silently. Someone raised the blind on the world to expose the spongy khaki of an army blanket.

I pull my neck down into my coat and pick up my cases, waiting to see which carriage the others get into. There are only two. Mr. Lochore and Mrs. Millar climb into the first, the two strangers into the second. I follow them like a fugitive. As I close the carriage door, the train grinds, stutters and moves forward.

The carriage is hot so I undo my coat and loosen the scarf around my neck. I'm tucked away at the back near the window and no one can see me. Feel more relaxed now, having achieved the most crucial part of my plan.

197

Condensation on the window makes it look frosted. I wipe a hole with my sleeve so that I can see out.

The countryside is yawning with dampness. It dribbles from the buildings, trees and fences. Transparent ovals, gliding to the ground, make it shine as though brushed with glycerine. People are stirring. Farmers herd their cows for milking. Cowshed lights twinkle and puffs of cow breath mushroom into the air. Dogs bark and wag. We pass a truck chugging along a metal road. The driver's huddled over the steering wheel, cigarette damp between his frozen lips. Inside the houses, I imagine babies yowling in their urine-soaked cots, women red-eyed and drowsy tying themselves into dressing gowns, bare feet tramping to bathrooms, heaters glowing, stoves turned on, pots clanking. . . .

They told me. At the breakfast table. That they're going to get married.

Happy we were, until then, eating poached eggs and talking, no one in a hurry because it was Sunday. It was one of those pleasant winter mornings when the sun was shining to create the illusion of summer, though the wind was icy cold. Mr. Wilson remarked on this and set our conversation alight.

"Reminds me of down south," he said, "when you get frosts heavy enough to curl your toes but by midday the sky's dead blue and the sun's warm if you keep out of the wind. Good working weather. Clean and brisk."

Kitty wasn't listening. She wasn't switched onto our chatter and if I'd had my wits about me, I'd have known she was brewing up to something. She had a different look about her, somehow soft and compliant and when she spoke, her voice drifted like soap bubbles.

"Harper, we've got something to ask you, dear," she said.

Ask me! With them both sitting there. Knowing?

"Ted and I are going to get married. We've decided. . . ."

Pause, while they scrutinized my face for reaction. Swallowed my surprise, choking, struggling as though over a large hunk of toast that I hadn't chewed properly.

"We wanted to ask you about it first before we made any definite arrangements because you're important to us. Me especially. We want you to feel happy about it. As happy as we are."

It came out pat as though she'd been studying the manuals. 'How to Tell Your Child of a New Marriage'. 'Explaining Step-Parents to Your Child'. Smiling, they were, though I could only see the eyes. It seemed that they'd turned into Cheshire cats, sparkling eyes and grinning mouths with nothing in between to hold them together.

"Well? What do you think?"

"I suppose it's a bit of a shock, lass," Mr. Wilson said. "Though you must've had some idea, eh? Not such a bad one, is it?"

They were leaning across the table toward me, willing me to take part in their happiness, perhaps even wanting to include me. The little voice inside me said, 'Smile, Harper'. So I did. Three Cheshire cats grinning at each other, all a long way off, none knowing exactly what the others expected of it.

"Say something, darling," said my mother.

"That's great," I said, swallowing, stretch-mouthed. "Just great."

I hoped that I sounded as though I meant it because they didn't seem to relax at all. What was I supposed to say? 'I hope you'll both be very happy?' 'Congratulations. When's the big day?' I felt bewildered, as though I was looking down at a finger that had been cut from my hand. As yet the pain hadn't seeped through the numbness but I knew that it would.

"Nothing'll change much," Mr. Wilson said. "We're really a family already. This'll just make things legal. Tidy it up a bit. Stop the neighbors gossiping."

He laughed and slapped Kitty's knee, winking at her. Awful to see him wink with that empty artificial eye.

"It'll be better for all of us," said Kitty.

I looked at her, my mother, and saw her as a stranger. She had already left me. For Mr. Wilson. The man I found. She preferred him to me. I supposed that it wouldn't mean my mother and me sharing ourselves with Mr. Wilson any more but that she'd toss me scraps of her time and affection as one tosses fatty bits of meat to a stray dog. How on earth would I manage without her?

"I knew she'd like the idea," said Mr. Wilson, patting my mother's hand. He turned to me. "Your mother was a bit worried that you wouldn't be very happy about it. We'll be a proper family now, Harper. I'm tickled pink. Aren't you?"

"It's great," I said again.

My mind was jammed with so many conflicting thoughts and feelings which it couldn't process, that that was the only remark it would produce.

"Are you sure, darling?" said my mother who couldn't accept the affirmative without query. "You're quite sure?"

"Of course she is," said Mr. Wilson.

"I told you. It's great," I said.

"We-ll," said my mother who likes to breed doubt in the minds of others. "If you're absolutely positive. . . ."

"It's what you want, isn't it?" I said, knowing perfectly well that she wouldn't change her mind. Not even for me. "I mean. What difference does it make what I think?"

She'd got it. The reaction. The grain of doubt. But she'd found someone in Mr. Wilson to counteract this tendency in her.

"Now Kitty," he said firmly. "Harper has said that she likes the idea, so that's enough. Don't go on at her. Give her time to get used to it."

"I want her to be sure, Ted, that's all," said my mother. "After all, she is my daughter. She's involved, too."

But she didn't really care whether I was sure or not. I knew that. She wanted my approval without opposition. She wanted my word, no matter how obliquely, that I wouldn't make a fuss.

"Of course she's involved," Mr. Wilson said. "That's why we've been discussing it. She thinks it's a great idea and so do I."

"Still, you never know with Harper," said my mother doubtfully, "quite what she thinks."

I thought, they're going to have a fight over me.

"When are you. . . ? When's it going to happen?" I said, afraid to mention the words marriage or wedding and sounding as though one of us was about to be admitted to hospital for major surgery.

"We haven't set a date," he said. "We wanted to talk to you first."

"Soon," said my mother.

I spent most of the day lying on my bed. I should have been deliriously happy. For the first time in my life, I was about to have a real acceptable family. A mother who was my parent and Mr. Wilson who would act as one. Two parents. A home. Security. A respectable little unit I could face the world with.

I liked Mr. Wilson, really. He took my side frequently in my fights with my mother. He calmed her, his quiet, placid nature balancing her 'freneticism', and I knew that here we lived more peacefully than we ever had before. But I felt resentful. Lonely. It had always been my mother and me. We had survived, the two of us, and I didn't see why we shouldn't continue to. And then I became confused because when it was just the two of us, I longed for a proper family. Now that I was about to have it, I no longer wanted it.

There was one thing I did want and that was their attention. I wanted them to focus everything on me but I didn't know how to achieve it. I'd tried. I'd shown off until I'd bored them silly. I'd behaved like a little kid until they'd remonstrated with me. I'd hung around glowering and sulking and brought my mother's anger down on me. Occasionally, I'd tried being grown-up but then they'd say things like, 'Don't interrupt, Harper, when you don't know what we're talking about'.

I supposed I might be jealous but there seemed to be no real place in their lives for me any longer. It was the two of them, joking, laughing, touching each other—and I, the outsider, not quite belonging, even when they remembered to include me. I couldn't sort it all out. My feelings or my situation. The only thing I knew was that my mother had found happiness, not through me but apart from me.

The sun came down in a wide shaft through the screen curtain and onto my bed. Warm, almost embryonic, the bed with the hollow where my body lay and my head nestled into the pillow. I read a while—Georgette Heyer's *The Spanish Lady*—but I didn't find it gripping the way I usually find her books.

I day-dreamed. About a rich family. One which had nothing to do with my mother or Mr. Wilson. I had rich and beautiful parents, brothers who spoiled me and a much older sister who was married and had a baby. We lived in a mansion with park-like grounds, a sweeping driveway and crazy paths leading through bush to a secluded swimming pool in a stream. There was a tennis court and a barbecue. I went to a private school and rode horses with such expertise that all the other girls envied me and, of course, it made me extremely popular with the handsome riding instructors. Each summer we travelled to foreign countries on the family yacht and every winter we went to Austria on a skiing holiday. It was there that I fell in love with a tall blond ski instructor. . . .

The afternoon whittled away and it was quite dark when Kitty came in and switched on the light.

"What're you doing, dear?" she said.

I didn't answer, but stretched and yawned.

"Come out by the fire. Anyway, I want you to set the table for dinner."

I stood up and ran my fingers through my hair.

She moved further into the room, scrutinizing my face.

"Harper, you look dreadful," she said. "You're so pale, dear. For goodness sake tidy yourself up a bit. Go and wash your face."

When she'd gone, I looked in the mirror. I thought, she can't stand me. She thinks I'm ugly.

We're on the edge of the city now and the world is properly awake. Country greenness has given way to the indiscriminately colored weatherboard and brick houses. The tracks run between rows of backyards, the ugly, not-to-be-seen parts of people's homes with sheds and outhouses, joined or separate, seeming to have been thrown and left to stand wherever they landed. The odd garment flaps damply from clothes lines, and fruit trees, whiskery pencil-strokes, struggle with the wind.

We stop frequently at suburban stations, and clusters of people, screwed up with the cold, fill the carriages. A fat man sits beside me and overflows into my seat. I draw away, closer to the window, turtle fashion, but he's not interested in me. He flicks open his newspaper.

I think about Kitty and Ted—Mr. Wilson. They'll be awake now. Mr. Wilson, in dressing gown and slippers, will be putting the kettle on for tea and Kitty will be stretching in her bed. I wonder whether they'll have discovered I'm missing, but I think not. They'll probably think I'm in the bathroom or out in the greenhouse looking at my orchids because one flowered unexpectedly and out of season the other day. When they do discover I'm missing they'll call the police. There'll probably be a radio announcement. . . .

'A fourteen-year-old girl has been missing from her home in

203

Ngaurimu since late last night or early this morning. The girl's name is Harper Catherine O'Leary and she's five feet four inches tall with long blond hair and green eyes. She's thought to be wearing blue jeans, a pale blue jersey under a red and gray checked coat and a natural wool scarf. If anyone has seen this girl or knows anything concerning her whereabouts, would they please get in touch with their nearest police station.'

. . . I'm biting my little fingernail. Anxious. At fault. Kitty won't go to work. They'll blame themselves. Each other. Kitty'll whip herself into an awful rage. I can see her, hair flying, eyes flashing, being irrational. And what she won't do to me when she gets her hands on me! Poor Mr. Wilson—Ted.

I said to him, "Don't you expect me to call you 'Dad'. You're not my father."

He said, "Of course not. I don't expect that. That'd be silly."

"What'm I supposed to call you, then? Mr. Wilson sounds stupid now."

Paused he did, looked at me with that one knowing eye.

"You call your mother Kitty. Why not call me Ted? After all, we're three grown-up people living in the same house. Harper and Kitty and Ted. I like the idea."

I did, too, but I pretended not to.

I knew she wasn't in the bedroom. It was too dark to distinguish anything—the outline of the windows, dressing table, the foot of my bed, her bed—yet I knew she wasn't there. I suppose it was the silence, so intense that I was aware of the absence of her breathing even though, in sleep, it has the delicacy of wood smoke curling into the sky.

All the old fears overcame me as I lay half-awake. As long as I can remember, if I woke in the night and she wasn't there, I'd panic. Short sobs instead of steady breathing, muscles clenched

204

all the way down my body, dry throat, wide eyes, afraid to call out in case it disturbed the evil thing lurking in the darkness. Had to force myself to control my fear. Wide awake, I thought, 'She's in the kitchen. A midnight snack for us. Just Kitty and me wrapped in our dressing gowns and an oasis of light, drinking cocoa and eating thick slices of toast and jam.'

Out of bed, quickly, seeing the solid lumps which were furniture, arms stretched out to the wardrobe for my dressing gown, knowing it by the feel of the fabric rather than seeing it. Careful to be quiet so as not to disturb Mr. Wilson. Inching out of the room, arms waving like antennae in front of me, I shuffled down the passage. I saw no light from the kitchen, but thought the door was closed.

It wasn't closed and she wasn't there. Not in the bathroom, either. Don't know why I went further down the passage because I didn't think for a moment she'd be in Mr. Wilson's room.

His door was open and it took me ages to distinguish the furniture but I stayed in the doorway because there were thrashing movements in his bed and the sound of heavy breathing. At first I thought he was having a nightmare so I waited, uncertain about what I should do. But then there were voices, soft murmurings so that I couldn't make out what they were saying. A man and a woman. Prickles all over me. It was Kitty. My mother. In Mr. Wilson's bed.

Stood there, shivering, feeling so lonely that I couldn't even cry. I wanted to call out to her but I didn't. They were moving in the bed, embracing, sighing, making love, and I knew better than to disturb them. I crept down the passage a few feet, hunched, biting my fingernails, not knowing what to do or where to go. I returned to the doorway. It was true. She was in Mr. Wilson's bed. I hated her. Both of them. Pounding, they were, he on top and she not minding. Blankets in heaps on the floor. I went hot. Sticky hands and perspiration on my forehead. The bedsprings creaked. I ran to my bedroom furious at their closeness and their rejection of me.

I'd never associated my mother with sexual activity before. It was strange to think of her in that capacity. I wondered what 'it' would be like. The jokes we told at school had now become focussed on a reality and I wanted to know more about this love between a man and a woman. How did she and Mr. Wilson get started? What did 'it' feel like? What I'd seen on television and in films was quite different from watching my own mother. I wished I hadn't seen it.

For a long time, I stood at the window staring at the night which was thick, black and almost tangible. I wondered whether they'd look different in the morning, whether I'd see any subtle signs to show what they'd been doing in the night. Couldn't bear the thought of them doing the things that we always did on a Monday morning, pretending to me that they weren't hiding anything. Hypocrites. I knew that they didn't love me.

Tight-curled in my bed, I made plans until my thoughts drifted into my fantasy world, to my Austrian ski instructor, and for the first time that I was aware of, my dreams were torrid and sexual.

When I woke up, damp and troubled, Kitty was there, in her bed, lying on her side away from me, head resting against an uplifted arm. She was sleeping peacefully.

It was time for me to go.

The sun is weak, filtering through the clouds. People pass me without a glance. The seat's wet and I can feel the dampness seeping through my jeans.

Two boys come toward me. Islanders, from the way they're dressed. About sixteen or seventeen. They're showing off, shouldering each other into the gutter, eyeing me and giggling. Hurriedly, I pick up my case and walk away, glancing surreptitiously over my shoulder to make sure that they're not following. They're still fooling and have forgotten my existence if they ever noticed it in the first place. I slow down. No one is interested in me.

· 21 ·

Funny how one can deceive oneself. Subconsciously I must have intended coming here all the time. Not once did I admit it to myself, though. My plans centered around Diana Pardon and Tony, around Mrs. Eagles with thoughts of her taking me in and eventually adopting me. I included Linda McLean in my scheme, too, because she seemed less of a drag in my memory after nearly a year passing without seeing her. I even drew into my fantasy the Turbetts and Mrs. Strong. In fact, I scraped up the courage to run away by projecting myself back into Rototui Street with everything much as it was before we had to leave, except for my mother. She was excluded.

But here I am, standing in front of this enormous apartment building gazing up at the penthouse plonked ludicrously on top like a too small hat on a fat man's head. My palms are sweaty and my nerves twang. Melting butter. My legs wanting to trickle away from me. But I'm compelled to go on up the gravel driveway, into the entrance hall and, I decide, because it will take longer, up the stairs.

Puffing, when I arrive at the top but not altogether from the exertion of having climbed twelve flights of stairs. Nervous, with my heart pounding to tell me so.

For a long time I stand staring at the lion-headed door knocker and the imitation Arabic carved wood panels in the door, wishing it would open and Eric would be standing there. I wonder should I use the knocker or should I press the button which immediately spills musical notes?

The knocker seems more matter-of-fact, more appropriate to my mood. I bang three times. It makes an awful din.

Eric opens the door and stands, mouth open, arms outstretched, surprise crushing anything he was about to say.

"Hello," I say, shuffling, feeling foolish.

"Harper!" he laughs. "Harper O'Leary. But what a surprise."

He folds me in his arms in an enormous hug. My face makes contact with the cool smoothness of his silk dressing gown and I'm reminded of how early it is. Then he pushes me back, holding me at arm's length.

"My goodness you've grown. Just look at you. I'd never have recognized you, you're so tall and slim. And beautiful."

He dances a little, a twitchy nightclub movement to cover our awkwardness and then his eyes fall on my suitcase.

"That looks like a school case to me," he says.

I nod. I'm incapable of speech.

He cocks his head to one side, considering.

"You should be at school, shouldn't you? Perhaps?"

"Yes."

It's such an odd sound that I clear my throat and repeat the word. He draws me into the hall and shuts the door. He cups my face in his hands.

"What have you done?" he says, looking straight into my eyes so that I have to blink. "Why are you here when you should be at school, Bluebird?"

"I-I-"

Fluttering. Not knowing what to say. To admit to running away would sound childish to this sophisticated man, who, now that I'm here, seems almost a stranger.

"I didn't feel like it today," I bluster, "so I decided to come and see you instead."

He laughs. That delicious soft sound with his head thrown back and his throat stretched to show all the sinews.

209

"Harper O'Leary, I believe you've run away. What on earth will Kitty say?"

Blushing. Feeling absurd.

"She won't care. She's getting married."

"Married?"

Suddenly he looks flustered, playfulness windswept from his face. It dawns on him that my visit is far more serious than just a friendly one, a harmless gesture of defiance to alleviate the boredom of the school term. He seems to anticipate something sinister in my appearance. A problem that will possibly involve him.

We're still in the hall, Eric leaning against the dark green embossed wallpaper, his shoulder nudging a red-mounted hunting print. For a moment I feel that I'll see no further into his apartment, that he'll open the door and throw me out.

"But you must be pleased," he says. "It must be so much better for Kitty having a man around. And for you. Aren't you happy to have a-a father?"

His eyes drop and so do mine. There's embarrassment between us. I wonder, should I say, 'I don't like him. He's not my father. You are and I want to live with you.' But we're saved from our discomfort by the door at the end of the hall which opens to release a gush of activity. A man appears, also in a dressing gown, and at the same time, a white Maltese terrier comes yapping along the carpet. She's followed by three tumbling balls of fluff that leap and lick as I bend to fondle them.

"Oh dear!" says the man. "I've let those bloody dogs out."

His voice is deep. I note that it's strangely unanimated. Not like other people's—Kitty's, for example—when they swear. Kitty sounds like factory hooters in full blast.

As the stranger and I eye each other, something claws anxiously at my insides. I hadn't expected to find that someone else had taken my place. With hostility, I stare at him. Tall he is. Much taller than Eric and lean. His hair's thin and his face long, sad, like a Basset hound. There's no change of expression as he clutches at his dressing gown. Immediately, I dislike this intruder.

"This's Mitzi," Eric says, picking up the mother dog.

"Come on, Eric. Bring your visitor in and have breakfast," the man says, his passive voice floating down the hall.

He disappears, closing the door.

I'd forgotten that spaces left by people are quickly filled by others, that situations change as rapidly as cloud, and sunshine moving across a lawn on a windy day.

I say, "I'm awfully sorry. I didn't know there'd be anyone else here. I would've phoned first only. . . . I didn't think. . . . I. . . ."

"That's Roland," Eric says. "He's a friend. You'll meet him in a moment."

"I suppose I'd better be going," I say, rubbing a puppy under my chin, making no effort to leave.

Eric ignores that remark and asks instead where I'm living these days.

"Out at Ngaurimu," I say. "With Mr. Wilson. He's a market gardener. That's who Kitty's going . . . going . . . to. . . ."

I stop, choked by the memory of Kitty and Mr. Wilson— Ted.

"It's beautiful out there," Eric says quickly, breezily to plug up the emotion I'm about to spill. "Anyway, come along. Roland's got breakfast ready and I bet you're hungry." He moves down the hall. "Bring those puppies, will you, Harper. I don't want them messing all over the carpet."

Gathering up the three puppies, I follow him into the lounge. Roland is sitting at the dining table and I resent his presence, the possessive, familiar way he fits into the place. He shouldn't be here. He's ruining everything.

"Roland, this's Harper," Eric says, chuckling, fluttering a

hand in my direction. "She should be at school but she's come to see me instead."

Roland shows no surprise. He's heard of me. I glare sulkily, furious to think that Eric has discussed me with him.

"Hello, Harper," says the deep monotone voice. "Taken a day off, have you?"

A sullen nod from me.

He doesn't smile. His face is almost comical with its unchanging hang-dog expression.

He tells me that he once took a day off when he was about my age. A circus had come to his town. He got six of the best from the headmaster and another beating from his father when he got home. Had a behind like minced steak after they'd finished with him, he said.

I'm about to respond but remind myself that I don't like him. A derisive snort instead, though I'd have liked to sympathize with him.

"Sit over there," Eric says pointing to a chair.

Looking at his watch, Roland says that he's been at Eric to come and have breakfast for almost twenty minutes. There's a mild growl in his voice as he says that he can't stand cold meals. Especially when he's gone to the trouble of preparing them. I can tell that he's only pretending to be angry.

Eric chuckles and helps himself to a slice of toast. So do I, lathering it well with marmalade. As Roland leans over to pour me a cup of coffee, I notice that his long fingers are embellished with large expensive looking rings. Mr. Wilson never wears rings. Eric does but they look good on him. Roland's look nice, too. His hands are attractive to watch.

There's something about his manner that makes me feel that we're old friends and that he's pleased to see me. It's difficult to sustain my dislike because he chats in that deep voice about things that interest me. Inside I want to laugh at him. Knows it, too. Deliberately doing it to make me feel welcome.

Scrunching on a piece of toast, I say, "I just called in for a minute, you know. I haven't come to stay. I'd better be going on as soon as I've finished this."

Roland's reply is what I'm fishing for. He raises his eyebrows and says that I mustn't go yet. I've just arrived. Why don't I stay for the day? He has to go to work in a minute but Eric doesn't have to hurry.

Eric looks doubtful.

"We-ll," he says, "I don't suppose you'd get back in time for school now anyway."

"Not unless she's jet propelled," Roland jokes, not a muscle changing the course of his expression.

"Don't encourage this sort of thing," says Eric, but he's smiling.

"I'm being practical," says Roland.

Eric makes a half-serious protesting noise then says that, yes, I must stay. For the day, at least.

"That's great," I grin, grateful to Roland.

I decide that I like him after all, in spite of first impressions. I justify my surliness by thinking that he must be one of those people who look unfriendly but who are really easy to get along with once you know them. I can see that his presence here is no threat to me. In fact, he seems to like me enough to possibly influence Eric into letting me stay. Forever. Hope he didn't notice how I felt about him to start with.

"Excuse me," he says, laying down his table napkin. "I must fly. Some of us have to work, you know."

As he rises, he asks me to come and see them again sometime soon. I nod. He doesn't know how soon, yet.

Eric asks about the shopping.

Leaving the table, I play on the floor with the puppies while they discuss the day's menu. If I didn't know the thing I do about them, the situation wouldn't give me a queasy feeling. It wouldn't have a quality of unreality about it. They'd seem like two ordinary people sharing an apartment. I concentrate on squeezing what I know out of my mind. But my mind is perverse. One of those men is your father and they're lovers, it says. I don't care, I retort. It doesn't matter to me. But there is a niggle. My recollection of Eric has played tricks. He's different than what I remember. The situation is different from what I expected.

"Okay then. Steak."

"And mushrooms," says Eric.

They're looking at me.

"What about Harper?"

"I think I'd better return her to her mother before dinner time," says Eric.

Infinitely small, I feel. Like a baby. And superfluous. He doesn't want me either.

Roland bends toward me. He's read my disappointment.

"Another time," he says. "Steak and mushrooms and chocolate cake."

He's kind. No wonder Eric likes him.

They go out of the room, still talking. A puppy chews my index finger and another jumps at me. The mother lies quietly, chin on floor, watching. I can hear voices coming from the bedroom and am tempted to listen at the door. But I don't. Fascinated, in a detached sort of way. I want to know what they're saying about me.

Louder now, the voices, and I know that they've shifted into the hall.

"Don't worry," I hear Eric say. "I'll get that. And some cornflakes. You like ordinary old cornflakes best, don't you?"

There's a teasing note in his voice and both men laugh. Sound fades as they move toward the front door. I didn't hear anything about myself. Don't know what they think. Disappointment. I'd been hoping that they'd been discussing me. My future.

214

Tossing backwards and forwards like a ball, the question of whether I should stay or not. But then, they don't really know, yet. I'll have to choose the moment carefully. When to tell Eric.

Soon he comes into the living room. He stands tall, blond, elegant. I'm smitten with adoration. He is the same person. The difference is in me. In the knowledge I have of him.

"Now Harper. Bluebird. What about another cup of coffee?"

He is the same, I insist. But no matter how hard I try, I can't revive the affinity, the lyricism that existed between us when I lived here.

I say, trying to bridge the gap, to please him, "I like Roland. He's nice."

"That's good. Roland likes you, too."

"Does he?"

Grinning. Flattered. I like to be liked. It makes me feel more confident. About living here. What they are won't make any difference to me.

I feel a surge of protectiveness toward them. I'd defend them against the snideness of catty, ignorant people. No one would dare to criticize them in front of me.

Eric goes to have a shower and to dress and I do the dishes. I wash and dry, remembering where everything belongs, happy in the old familiar surroundings. From the bedroom comes the sound of his voice and I know he's talking on the telephone.

Kitty.

He's telling her where I am.

He's deceiving me.

My future wobbles. Crashes.

He definitely doesn't want me.

When he comes out, we sit and talk but our conversation clatters around us. Words dropping into an empty bucket.

"Aren't you going to work today?" I say in my pleasantest voice, still hoping to win him over, to convince him that he

215

needs me, that I'll be no trouble. "You don't have to stay because of me."

He says, "Not today. I don't have a visit from you everyday, Bluebird. This's a special occasion."

I smile my ethereal smile to show my appreciation of his sacrifice for I know now that that's what it is.

"Were you talking to Kitty a little while ago?"

"Yes. I thought she'd be worried."

He moves to tousle my hair the way he used to in the old days, but withdraws before he touches me.

"What'd she say? Was she mad?"

"A bit, I think. But she hadn't notified the police which was lucky. I caught her just in time."

He's relieved. Relieved at having sorted it out. Relieved at not being involved after all. And now that he's certain of his own immunity he's not nearly so interested. In me. I'm sorry for myself and for a few minutes have trouble biting back the tears in my throat. I'm sure, even if Roland were eliminated, that my future isn't with Eric. My father.

He shows me a set of Edwardian pewter mugs and a painting he's just bought. The painting hangs in the corner above the solid round ivory Buddha and cost him eighteen hundred and fifty dollars.

"What's it meant to be?" I say, screwing up my eyes, trying to make something out of the red and black splodges with the nut of yellow light in the right-hand corner.

"It's not meant to be anything," he says, gazing at it, transported into some mystical state through its obscure message.

We stand silently, he uplifted, me bewildered, squirming at my obtuseness, the painting creating an even greater rift between us. I think of the autumn-toned collie with the pheasant and the sheafs of wheat hanging above the fireplace at Mr. Wilson's and decide that I like it far better.

As the morning wears on, I feel conspicuously clumsy and

shabby among all this elegance. I'm afraid to touch anything in case I break it. Afraid to relax in case I spill something. Eric's charming, gracious, as attentive as ever I remember but it seems that we have nothing in common and our incompatibility grows as the day does.

It would be easier, I think, if Roland were here with us. He's relaxed, cheerful, spilling jokes over the immaculate white carpet and polished furniture so that they seem less remote, less formal and frightening.

And, all the time, I'm comparing Eric with the easy, informative chats that Mr. Wilson and I have, even though I know this to be unfair.

"See that ring around the sun, Harper?" Mr. Wilson would say as I followed him around the farm, probably with a rake or a hoe slung over my shoulder. "That means rain. Did you know that? The sun's rays are trying to get through the moisture in the atmosphere. It's what is known as refraction."

I see his work-worn fingernails, skin around the edges dried orange peel and the lines at the corners of his eyes. Sparrows' footprints. I hear his even-tempered voice deflecting the verbal blows that my mother levels at me and see the twinkle in his eye as he calms her down. He's not as elegant as Eric. I don't admire him in the same way or love him but he's easy to be with as Roland seems to be. There's not the awkwardness with Mr. Wilson that I'm feeling now with my father.

But I don't want to go back.

To Ngaurimu.

To them.

After lunch, Eric turns on the television. There's nothing else to do. It's too late. To talk about us. All day I've wanted to tell him that I know he's my father. Difficult it's been to find the right moment. Now it no longer matters.

He hasn't mentioned it. He's avoided anything personal. Barely enquired about Kitty or who she's going to marry. It seems that he wants to keep as far away from our lives as possible. It's all her fault, really. She's always been horrible to Eric, saying rude things and sending back my birthday presents. I wonder should I mention the presents but decide not to. It's too embarrassing.

We sit and make efforts at conversation which dribbles lamely for a while and then dies because we can't find anything in common. I can tell that Eric's run out of appropriate things to say but I tell him more about school and he tells me again about his mother and what happened when he went to school. The American soap opera fills the gaps like boring background music. Someone has a miscarriage and someone else says it's just as well because it wasn't the husband's child. Eric brings me a lemon drink and chocolate biscuits. On television a girl walks out into the snow and collapses under a tree. I ask Eric what time Roland comes home. He says about five-thirty. The girl's almost covered up with snow. Eric says that Roland has a boat and that if Kitty will let me, I can stay with them for holidays. We'd go fishing and for picnics. I say that that would be neat and I mean it.

Later in the afternoon, he phones Roland. Their conversation is love talk even though he doesn't use one word of endearment. I don't feel jealous or rejected. Just a little sad. For us both.

When he's finished speaking on the telephone he looks at his watch.

"Good heavens," he says, fluttering a hand in that old manner of his. "It's ten past three and I promised Kitty I'd put you on the four o'clock train. Gather your things, Bluebird. We'll have to fly."

So I'm to go back.

To them.

Kitty and Ted—Mr. Wilson.

Eric looks at me.

"Cheer up," he says. "It's not the end of the world."

218

He looks around for something to distract me. To bribe? Perhaps to comfort me.

"How would you like a puppy?"

I stare, disbelieving, face cracking with pleasure.

"Are you sure? I mean . . . gosh! For me?"

"Who else but my Bluebird. Which one would you like?"

"Oh heavens," I laugh. "I don't know."

I stare at them, sheep-skin balls curled in sleep.

"Those two are bitches," he says, "and the other one's a dog."

He bends and tickles its tummy. The dog wakes, grumbles sleepily and chews his finger.

"That one," I say. "I'll take the dog."

He picks it up and hands it to me.

"Will Kitty let you have it?"

"We-ll. She might make a fuss to start with but Mr. Wilson'll think it's okay. He'll let me have it."

"Fine. Come on then, Bluebird."

He takes my case and bustles me out of the apartment. On the way to the station I say, "I know what I'm going to call him."

"What?" says Eric.

"Robson."

He grins. He's pleased, I think.

I catch the four o'clock train, the dog tucked away under my coat so that no one will see him. Eric says that it was super to see me, that we must spend more time together now that we've found each other. In a joking voice, he says that I mustn't run away anymore. Instead, I can stay with him for weekends and holidays. He'll get in touch with Kitty about it. Think he means it. Hope so, anyway. He waits until the train pulls out. The last I see of him is his lean body, erect on the platform, arm stretched waving me goodbye.

It's an unhappy feeling but Robson intervenes. He whimpers and then piddles all over my skirt. I can't do a thing because someone might discover that I have him here. I sit uncomfortably feeling the hot trickle down my legs. It quickly turns cold. I'll have to stay like this all the way home. Smell awful by the time I get there. He snuggles into my stomach and goes to sleep.

I lean back and watch winter flashing past the window. I wonder what sort of reception I'll get. I imagine it will be stormy but I don't worry about Robson. Mr. Wilson will defend him.

"Harper needs something of her own," he'll say. "Look at this little fella. He'll be no trouble."

I visualize our kitchen. Lights on because it will be dark by the time I arrive. Dinner cooking. Perhaps burning because no one will be thinking much about food. The windows will be steamed up. Like Kitty. Anger will make her flushed, aggressive, and she'll home in on me straight away. Ted will be there, though, calm, pit-pitting on his pipe, ready to referee.

Scream at me, Kitty will, the moment I walk in the door.

"Where've you been? What did you do it for? I've been sick with worry all day. I've got a good mind to thrash you."

Ted will blow the whistle..He'll say things like, "Now, now Kitty. Calm down. You know perfectly well why she did it. She had to see her father again. Harper's had a lot of sorting out to do so don't go on at her."

Ashamed, I'll feel with Mr. Wilson sticking up for me and my mother in a state.

But Kitty, because she loves me, will throw herself at me. As she crushes me, she'll say. "My God, Harper. I could kill you for putting me through today. Honestly! I don't know whether to beat you to death or to hug you to death."

I can't wait to get home.

"Hurry up train," I whisper.